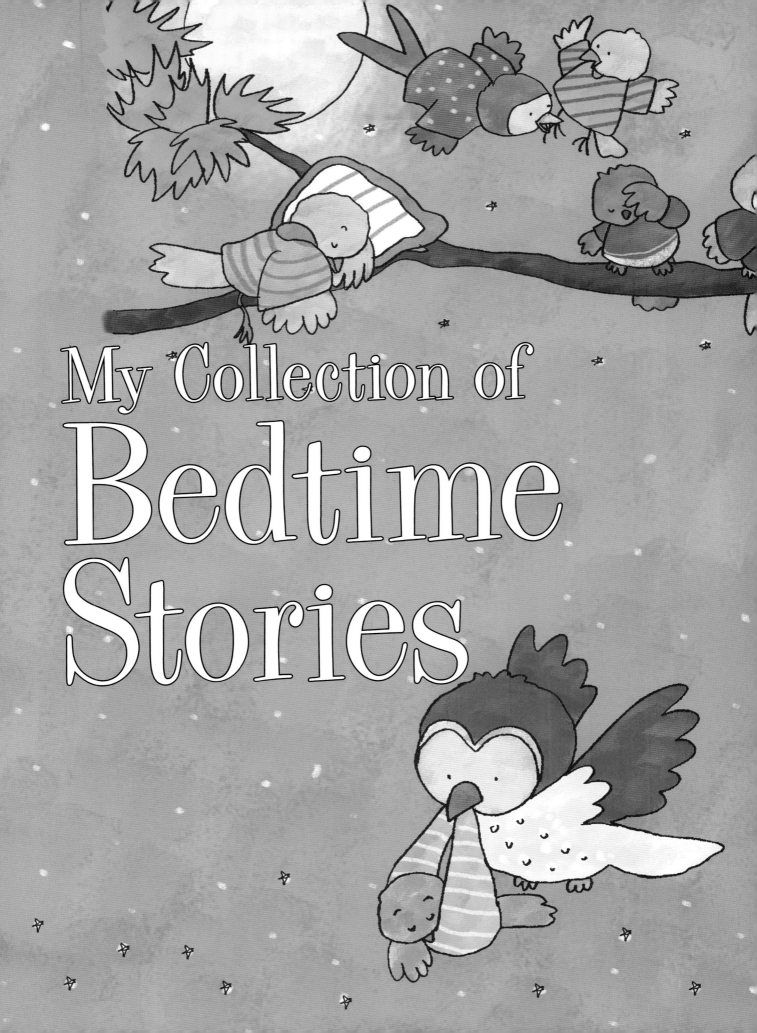

My Collection of
Bedtime
Stories

Contents

Contents contd.

Contents contd.

The Wee Island Of Loch Noddie

Little Red Mac and his friend Tam O'Tatie walked down by the shores of Loch Noddie.

"I've heard it said," Tam O'Tatie spoke very seriously, "that music can bring the Monster out of the Loch!"

So Tam O'Tatie took out his bagpipes and began to play. And while he marched to and fro playing fit to burst, his friend Little Red Mac kept a sharp look out across the lake, just in case the Monster appeared.

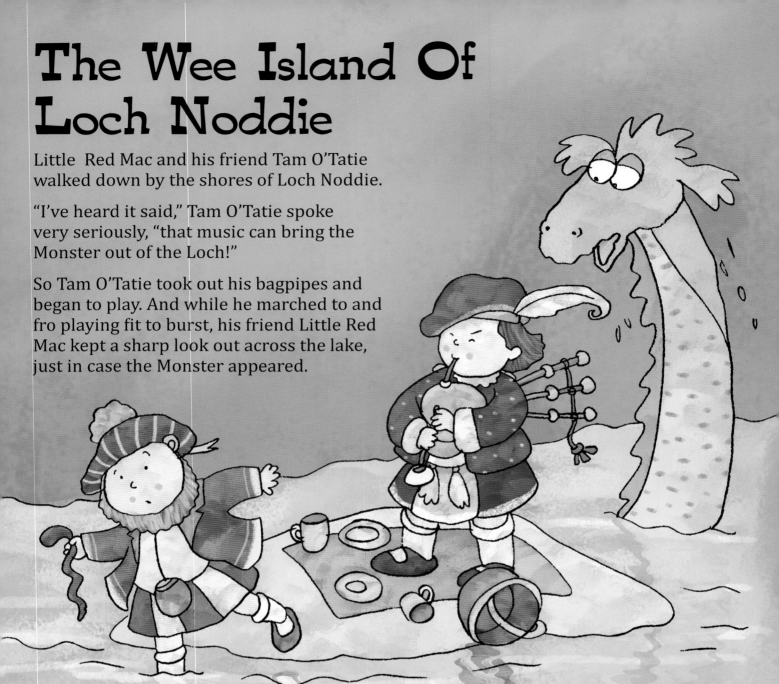

"Piping makes me feel hungry!" said Tam O'Tatie, pausing for breath.

'Then let's find a place for a picnic." said Little Red Mac, (as he always carried a basket full of food wherever he went).

So they waded out to a tiny island which neither of them had ever noticed before.

"This must be a new island." said Little Red Mac as he climbed up the side and got on the top.

"I know a tune called 'The Wee Island Of Loch Noddie," said Tam O'Tatie after they had eaten their picnic. "I shall play it for you on the bagpipes!"

No sooner had Tam O'Tatie started to play, than the new island slowly sank into the water, and an awful groaning noise came from the loch.

"It must be the Monster!" yelled Little Red Mac as he made for the shore.

"You silly man!" Tam O'Tatie said . "It's my bagpipes! Now what do you think it was?"

Congratulations, Mr Tappit!

"Tomorrow," said Mr Tappit the toy-maker, "I shall have been making toys for fifty years!" and he locked up his toy shop and went home for tea.

All the toys in the shop overheard what Mr Tappit had said. "We'll have a party tomorrow." said the baby doll.

"With presents!" said Teddy.

"And fireworks!" cried a shelf full of toys.

"We could have all three!" shouted the wind-up toys. "A party, presents and fireworks!"

"Don't forget a great big cake!" squeaked the tiny clockwork mouse.

"Let's get busy at once." said Teddy, and the toys gathered round.

By next morning, everything was ready.

Mr Tappit unlocked his toy shop as usual and stepped inside - and there in the middle of the floor, was the biggest cake he had ever seen.

All of a sudden there was a pop and a loud bang, and toys of all shapes and sizes jumped out of the gigantic cake.

Some of them had presents, some of them had cards, and one of them was holding a beautiful iced cake.

"Congratulations, Mr Tappit!" all the toys cried as they waved flags and threw streamers.

"What a surprise." laughed Mr Tappit quite out of breath. "You've made me very happy!"

"We're having fireworks tonight!" squeaked the tiny clockwork mouse as he scampered off to eat his cake.

Silver Lightning

Silver Lightning was the fastest train on the tracks. His engine was shining silver with blue and red flashes down the side.

On journeys, Silver Lightning sped from city to city so fast, that all folks saw when he whizzed past, was a blur!

"What an amazing train." the passengers said. "Silver Lightning can drive himself - he doesn't need a driver or a guard!"

"But I do!" cried Silver Lightning, and a big tear rolled down his gleaming paintwork. "I'm so lonely all by myself!"

So the man in charge of the railway found Silver Lightning his own driver and his own guard, who had nothing to do but ride everywhere on the special silver train and keep him happy!

Three Busy Workmen

Three busy workmen were digging a very deep hole in the road, when quite by accident their drill hit a water-pipe.

Soon everything was soaking wet and water was spurting in all directions.

"How on earth did that happen?" asked Jim.

"I think it was my fault!" said John.

"Can't be helped," said Joe "let's have our lunch!"

So the three busy workmen sat down and opened their lunch-boxes.

"Oh dear!" groaned Jim as he took out rulers and pencils and felt-tipped pens. "I've picked up my little girl's school-case by mistake!"

Then John opened his lunch box, and he'd picked up the wrong case as well - it was packed full of his little boy's school-books.

"I'd better look in mine," laughed Joe, and he began to blush. His wife had handed Joe her make-up case by mistake, with all her lipsticks and hairsprays!

"This means we have no lunch at all! cried the three busy workmen.

"If you promise to mend the pipe and stop all the water leaking," shouted the man from the sandwich shop nearby, "I'll make lunch for all three of you!" And the three busy workmen did just that!

The Bathroom Battle

Peter's mum was in a hurry one night at bathtime.

She rubbed and scrubbed Peter in double quick time, before he could blink he was washed, dried and tucked up tight in bed.

Back in the bathroom, all the toys were left alone on the shelf.

"It's not fair," said the penguin, "no-one has had time to play with us in the bath tonight!"

"Does that mean we shan't get bathed until tomorrow?" quacked the yellow duck.

"I love bath water!" cried the little blue fish. "Especially when it's full of bubbles."

"So do I!" barked the seal. "I hate being dry."

"Then we must do something about it!" the toy sailor said as he stood on the edge of the bath and spoke to them all. "I can turn on the taps, but I need a little help."

"I can use the end of my tail," said the whale. "I'll turn on the hot tap and you can do the cold tap," he told the sailor.

"Plug's in the plug hole!" said the little blue fish, as he swam quickly out of the way of the hot water.

It wasn't long before the bath was almost full. The seal put his flipper into the water -just to make sure that it wasn't too hot for the toys.

When the penguin gave the signal everyone dived in, and the sailor very kindly launched the boats and a whole family of ducks into the bath water.

"Let's have bubbles!" sang the whale at the top of his voice.

"Better still," barked the seal as he dived beneath the water, "let's have a bubble battle!"

Pretty soon everywhere was covered in soft white foam. There were big blobs of bubbles on the bathroom walls, and a pool of water all over the floor.

The whale threw a tail full of bubbles at the sailor, and the penguin and the seal filled the sailing boats to the brim.

"Quiet, someone IS coming!" yelled the sailor. Quick as a flash, the little blue fish dived down and pulled out the plug.

"This bathroom's been left a mess!" said Peter's dad as he opened the door. "Better get it cleaned up before Mum sees it!"

So he dried all the toys and put them back on the shelf.

The penguin, who was standing next to the seal, gave him a little nudge. "How about another bathroom battle tomorrow night?" he said.

Harriet's Wish

"I wish I had a playhouse." said Harriet, one day. "Then I could sit inside and just pretend!" and off she went

"Did you hear that?" whispered her dad.

"I did!" replied Harriet's mum just as quietly.

"If Harriet wants a playhouse, I shall build her one!" said her dad, quite determined.

So away he hurried to buy lots of wood, and to see if he needed any new tools.

"Are you sure Harriet really wants a playhouse?" mum shouted after him. But dad was already on his way to the timber yard.

It took simply ages to build the playhouse, with dad hammering and banging in nails every time Harriet left the house.

At long last it was finished, and mum and dad called Harriet into the garden to take a look.

Harriet was speechless and held her breath for a very long time, which made her mum look worried.

"That's not what I wanted!" cried Harriet shaking her head. So she ran indoors and came back with a picture of her playhouse in a book.

"Is that all," gasped her dad as he fell back into a garden chair.

"I want a playhouse just like that!" said the little girl, and she held up the book.

Now Harriet has the playhouse she really wanted - and dad has a brand new tool shed that he built himself!

The Penguins Join The Party

Chrissy, Sissy and Missy were sisters. They lived with their brother Sidney on an iceberg in the Atlantic Ocean.

One day, a ship taking passengers on a cruise stopped right next to the penguin's iceberg.

The people on board the cruise ship had never seen penguins before, especially one in a red waistcoat! So they leaned over the side and began to take video films and photographs.

"Do you mind being stared at?"

Chrissy, Sissy and Missy asked their brother Sidney.

"Not one bit!" said Sidney as he straightened his bow-tie.

So the four little penguins posed for the cameras until it grew dark.

Late that night, Chrissy, Sissy, Missy and Sidney heard music. It came from the brightly lit cruise-ship.

"Come on girls!" said Sidney. "It sounds like a party, so let's join in!"

So Chrissy, Sissy, Missy and Sidney jumped off their iceberg, swam over to the ship and clambered up on deck.

"Welcome aboard!" yelled the captain above the noise. "Today we stared at you, now it's your turn to stare at us. Come and join the party!"

Randolph The Reindeer

Randolph the Reindeer was extremely shy. While the other reindeer trotted through the trees holding their heads high and tossing their antlers from side to side - Randolph stood quietly nibbling the moss on the ground, with his head down.

"You're too timid, Randolph!" bellowed the other reindeer as they leapt through the woods. "Be a show-off like us!"

But Randolph pretended not to hear, he just went on nibbling the moss on the ground with his head down.

Then from beyond the trees came the shouts of children as they tobogganed down the snowy hillside.

"I'd love to join in," sighed Randolph, "but I'm far too shy!"

Then as Randolph began to nibble the moss on the ground with his head down, he came across a woollen hat. Next he found a mitten, then a long scarf.

All at once Randolph's nose began to twitch, and without thinking he held his head high and began to look around. There in a clearing on the edge of the trees lay a little boy by the side of his toboggan.

"I've hurt my leg and I can't walk!" the little boy cried.

So Randolph knelt down, and the little boy slipped his arms round the reindeer's neck and climbed on his back.

Very soon he was back home safely, thanks to Randolph. "You're a hero!" said the little boy.

This made Randolph feel so proud, that he lifted up his head and tossed his antlers from side to side - just like the other reindeer!

The Baby Bird's Bedtime

It was late afternoon and all the baby birds were practising flying.

"I can fly upside-down!" chirped a young robin.

"Can you dive from the top of the poplar tree, then brake just before you hit the ground?" asked one daring little thrush who had tried it several times.

"Look at us!" cried nine of the tiniest sparrows, as they flew close together overhead.

Just then, a strange little beak and two big eyes appeared from inside the trunk of the poplar tree.

"Hi everybody!" said a squeaky little voice. "I'm Ollie, can I play with you?

The baby birds stopped what they were doing at once and gathered around.

"You're new here" chirped the robin.

"Not exactly," Ollie replied. "I live in that hollow tree, and I've been here all the time."

"It's getting rather late for you to play." said one of the bluebirds. "Soon it will be dark!"

Poor Ollie looked very disappointed as he had just made so many new friends.

Then all of a sudden he thought of a wonderful idea.

"Why not stay over with me tonight?" cried Ollie.

So off flew the little birds came back wearing pyjamas. (One or two of the really young ones brought their blankets and pillows.)

"It's so exciting," sang the robin. "I've never stayed up all night before!"

At first everything went wonderfully well. The baby birds fluttered in and out of the branches, playing tag in the twilight.

But when darkness fell, they kept bumping into one another, and the thrush almost fell off his perch onto the ground below!

Ollie could see that his new friends were getting rather tired, so off he flew and came back with a tray of snacks and nice things to nibble.

"We're having a midnight feast!" whispered one of the sparrows, his head nodding onto his pillow.

Soon all the baby birds were falling asleep - some of them looked really uncomfortable.

"Why are you still wide awake, Ollie? the robin asked drowsily.

"It's because I'm an OWL, and we stay up all night long!" smiled Ollie, and he took all the sleepy little birds back to their warm nests.

Gordon's New House

Gordon the Gorilla was looking for a new house. So he rang up the man who sold really nice houses.

As you can see the house turned out to be a bit on the small side for Gordon.

I think that Gordon forgot to tell the man who sold really nice houses, that he was a gorilla.

"I have the perfect place for you, Mr Gordon." said the man who sold really nice houses. "It has a bright red roof, two tall chimneys and a smart white fence."

"Sounds just the job!" grunted Gordon.

"If you like it, Mr Gordon," said the man who sold really nice houses, "I'll be round straight away and you can pay me all your money!"

Belinda, The Circus Star

"I'm off to join the circus and be a star!" announced Belinda the rag-doll one morning at breakfast.

"For ever?" gasped the soldier doll.

"No silly!" Belinda sniffed. "Just for one day."

"One day!" all the toys laughed out loud. "How can you be a circus star in just one day?"

"Easy," said Belinda, "the clowns will teach me, you see!" and off she went.

At first the clowns were thrilled to see Belinda, because they thought the rag-doll was charming and very, very pretty, and every single one of the clowns wanted to teach her their tricks.

"I don't want to do tricks." said Belinda quite snappy. "I want to walk a tight-rope!"

"A tight-rope?" this surprised all the clowns.

"How about juggling instead?" asked one of them.

"Riding a unicycle is good fun!" suggested another.

Then all the clowns stood in front of Belinda. "We should never allow a beautiful rag-doll like yourself, to swing on a trapeze, or ride bareback, or walk a tight-rope- it's far too dangerous - and that's final!" they shouted.

"Rubbish!" Belinda yelled back as she stamped her feet. "I've already told my friends that I am going to walk a tight-rope and be a star - and that's final too!"

Whatever was to be done?

The clowns liked Belinda very much and didn't want to disappoint her, in spite of her bad temper that day.

"There is one way you can learn to walk the tight-rope without being in any danger at all!" said the clown with the big feet.

"Show me! Show me! Do, do, do!" shouted Belinda, very impatient, and so they did!

Belinda the rag-doll walked up and down the tight-rope all that day. She wore sparkling tights and a silver star on her head, and when the toys came to call for her that night, she showed them what she could do. "But Belinda," said the toys, "your tight-rope is only a few inches off the ground!" and they all burst out laughing!

"I agree," and Belinda smiled her prettiest and most charming smile, "but I did learn to walk a tight-rope and I am a circus star!" Then she bowed, still wearing her sparkling tights and silver star!

The Bear Who Drove The School Bus

On certain days when the regular driver had a day off, Barnaby would drive the school bus.

Now on those days when Barnaby drove the bus to school, he picked up his young animal friends at stops all along the forest road.

One day, as his last passenger climbed aboard, Barnaby got back into the driving seat - and the bus would not start.

However hard Barnaby tried, he could not start the engine!

"Hurrah!" yelled one of the raccoon twins. "Let's take the day off!"

So before Barnaby could stop them, all the young animals had jumped off the bus and rushed into the woods to play hide and seek.

"This is very naughty of you all!" shouted Barnaby, trying to sound gruff. "Come back at once!" and his voice echoed through the trees.

All the rest of that morning, poor Barnaby ran round in circles trying to catch the young animals. Every so often he would glimpse a couple of them peeking from behind a tree trunk.

Time passed and Barnaby began to feel hungry. "It must be almost dinner time!" he said out loud.

Then, as if from nowhere, all Barnaby's little animal passengers appeared.

"I'm very hungry!" cried one little fox cub.

"I'm hungry and thirsty too!" said a small squirrel.

"Take us back to school for our dinner!" the animals shouted all at once.

"I might have some food in my bag," said Barnaby, as he led them back to the bus - but all he could find was a packet of cough sweets and some rather old biscuits.

"We want our dinner!" "We want our dinner!" the animals began to chant, and they banged their feet loudly on the bus floor.

Just at that moment, a big car-transporter drew alongside the school bus.

"Need a lift?" asked the driver.

"I need lots of lifts" laughed Barnaby.

So Barnaby and the driver put a few of the animals into each car on the transporter.

"First stop school!" shouted the driver.

"Just in time for dinner!" yelled the little animals.

Dottie's In Fashion

Winter was coming and the weather was getting colder, so Dottie the dormouse went to the store to buy a new coat.

"Choose something sensible that is comfortable and warm." suggested her cousin Dora.

"Not likely!" scoffed Dottie.

"My new coat will be the latest fashion!" Then Dottie saw it - the most fashionable coat in the whole world!

"I'll take it!" Dottie yelled at the top of her voice. "Wrap it up at once!"

"Aren't you going to try it on?" asked her cousin Dora as she gazed open-mouthed at Dottie's new coat "It looks rather thin!"

But Dottie didn't hear her, she was far too busy trying on a pair of high-heeled boots to match.

"They look very unsuitable for wet, winter weather." said Dora under her breath as she followed Dottie out of the store.

During the night it turned very cold. The north wind blew and it started to snow, and it went on snowing and snowing and snowing.

When Dottie and Dora looked out of their window the next morning, the whole world was white.

"Get a move on Dottie!" cried Dora, who was already dressed in her warm jacket and boots.

I'll need time to button my coat up!" snapped Dottie. "Then it will take me quite a while to lace up my boots!"

So Dora went out to play in the snow with her friends.

At long last Dottie was ready. She stepped outside in her high heeled fashionable boots and fell flat on her back!

Now Dora and her friends were having a great time throwing snowballs and building a snowman.

But the snow was cold and wet, and very soon poor Dottie felt frozen in her fashionable coat.

"It's so c-c-c-cold, and my t-t-t-toes ache!"

"Let's get you inside." said cousin Dora shaking her head. "You need warm clothes on a day like this, not fashionable ones!"

"You're right!" agreed Dottie as she thawed out in front of a warm fire.

"Tomorrow we'll both go shopping and you can choose some sensible clothes for me, Dora. And I'll pack my fashionable coat and boots away until spring!"

Matt's Coffee Morning

Matt the Bat was feeling lonely. "I need to make new friends." he squeaked as he flitted across the night sky.

"My problem is," he told a passing owl, "each time I introduce myself, everyone screams and runs away!"

"I understand," nodded the owl wisely. "When people see a bat they think of witches and broomsticks and Halloween."

"Got it in one!" piped Matt. "They think of skeletons with rattling bones, and ghosts that jump out at you and shriek and groan!"

"Enough!" hooted the owl. "You're scaring me stiff!"

"Didn't mean too!" said Matt the Bat. "But what can I do?"

"Have a coffee morning!" suggested the owl. "Put a notice on your door inviting anyone passing to come in for coffee and cake. But remember, be sure to have it in the daytime!"

"What a clever old owl you are!" and Matt the Bat smiled as he flitted off home.

Now when visitors came to Matt's house the next day to join him for coffee and cake - they were in for a surprise.

There was Matt in his neat little house serving coffee and cake in his best frilly apron, UPSIDE-DOWN, but don't forget that Matt is a bat!

Buggy Races

"Would you like to race me down to the beach?" the Hare asked the Tortoise.

"Not really," muttered the Tortoise. "You'll win as usual!"

"That's true," said the Hare in a kind voice. "I'm sorry you always lose, it can't be much fun!"

But one day, the Hare found a way to race the Tortoise that would be fair and lots of fun too.

Come and look what I have found?" called the Hare to the Tortoise, who was slowly plodding over the sand hill towards the beach.

Now the two friends can race against each other all day, and something tells me that the Tortoise might win this time!

Gussie The Ginger Cat

Gussie the Ginger Cat made up her mind one day to catch every single mouse in the house.

So she fetched the biggest, tastiest, smelliest piece of cheese she could find, and put it inside a bag.

Now Gussie's bag had a string round the top. "When this bag is full of mice," sniggered Gussie, "I shall pull the string so tightly, that not one of them will escape."

But what Gussie didn't know, was that her bag had a big hole in the bottom.

So one by one, the crafty mice scampered into the bag, picked up the cheese and carried it out through the hole at the other end.

"Better luck next time Gussie!" giggled the mice, their mouths full of tasty cheese.

Matching Hats

Four tiny field mice went to playschool for the very first time.

"I want to paint!" said the first one.

"I want to make a model!" said the second.

"I want to sing and dance!" said the third.

"And I want milk and biscuits!" said the fourth.

While they were at playschool, each one of the tiny field mice had painted a picture, made a model, had danced round in a ring and sung a song about a farmer.

And all four tiny field mice had eaten a plateful of iced biscuits and shared a glass of milk with four curly straws.

At last it was time to go home, and the four tiny field mice went to find their hats.

"That's not my hat!" shouted the first one.

"That's not my hat!" shouted the second.

That's not my hat!" shouted third.

"Our hats must match!" shouted the fourth.

So can you help the field mice sort out their hats? They really are in a muddle!

The Farmer's Barn

One fine morning in autumn, a farmer and his wife were strolling through the fields looking at their corn crop.

"We've never had such a good harvest, dear!" said the farmer happily. "There'll be plenty of corn for us and all our friends. In fact, there'll be enough left over to feed the birds through the long winter."

"We'll give a party." suggested the farmer's wife. "In fact, my dear, I'll ask my cousins from over the hills and faraway."

So the farmer and his wife sent out invitations. Then they got busy in the farmhouse kitchen and made lots of delicious things to eat.

They set the food out in one of their fields under the shade of a tree. Soon neighbours began to arrive, and last of all came the cousins from over the hills and faraway.

It wasn't very long before everyone tucked into the lovely food and seemed to be having a good time. It was then the farmer and his wife noticed that the cousins from over the hill and faraway looked a bit glum. "Whatever is the matter?" asked the farmer.

"There must be something wrong with my food!" said the farmer's wife, and she tasted a piece of pie to make sure.

"The food is fine, thank you," the cousins from over the hills and faraway replied quietly. "But this year our crops have failed, and we have no corn to eat or save in our barns for winter."

"Don't worry!" cried the farmer.

"There's plenty here for all. Take as much as you like home with you, and then come back for more!"

At this, the cousins from over the hills and faraway cheered up considerably and began to enjoy the party.

When, at last, the food was finished and all the pots cleared away, the cousins from over the hills and faraway took a stroll round the farm, and would you believe it, for the second time that day, their faces began to look glum. "Look at your barns," they said to the farmer and his wife.

"They're falling to bits, you'll have nowhere to store your corn this winter!"

Now it was the farmer's turn to look glum. "Not to worry!" said the cousins from over the hills and faraway.

We'll stay a few days and repair your barns for you. It will be our way of saying thank you for giving us the corn.

The Tired Little Monkey

The smallest monkey at the zoo was very fond of Norah, the zookeeper's wife.

"It's because you spoil him so much," the zoo keeper grinned.

"I can't help it," Norah smiled as she lifted the little monkey up in her arms. "He's so cuddly and sweet, and he's just a baby!"

Now the little monkey liked nothing better than to follow Norah around all day long as she worked in the zoo.

"Can you carry me?" the little monkey asked Norah one afternoon. "My legs are tired!"

So for the rest of that afternoon, Norah took the little monkey around the zoo on her back.

"I do like this!" cried the little monkey. "I can see everything from up here, and I'm not a bit tired!"

"But I am!" whispered Norah under her breath (because she didn't want to upset the little monkey).

It took poor Norah twice as long to do all her jobs in the zoo, because the little monkey kept hugging her tightly round the neck and tickling her ears.

"Can we do this everyday?" begged the little monkey, and Norah gave a big sigh.

Early next morning the zoo keeper went into town to buy a pushchair- it was Norah's idea!

So now that little monkey is pushed around the zoo. He never gets tired, and neither does Norah!

43

Pippin Has The Measles

Ma and Pa Bramley were looking rather worried. Pippin, their pet pig, felt poorly.

"Have you been eating green apples from my orchard ?" asked Pa.

"Not one !" sniffed poor Pippin.

"Have you been drinking from muddy puddles?" asked Ma, because she had often watched Pippin do this when she thought no one was looking.

"We must send for the doctor," Ma and Pa decided, "he'll be sure to know what's the matter!"

By the time the doctor arrived, Pippin was covered in tiny red spots.

"Measles!" the doctor nodded wisely. "You have a pig with the measles!"

"You must stay in the kitchen with me!" announced Ma Bramley.

"Then you will be warm and dry, and I can make sure that you have plenty of warm bread and milk with brown sugar on top!"

Pippin quite liked the sound of this, so she trotted into Ma Bramley's kitchen and settled down in front of the fire.

It wasn't long before Pippin the pig began to feel a bit better, although she was still covered in bright red spots.

Some of the children in the valley heard about their friend Pippin and came to see how she was feeling.

"It's good to see you all," snuffled Pippin as she trotted towards the kitchen door.

"STOP RIGHT WHERE YOU ARE!" cried Ma Bramley. "You'll have all these nice children covered in spots and in no time at all the whole valley will catch the measles!"

"Did the doctor say when I could go out?" asked Pippin.

"Exactly one week from now, and not a moment before!" replied Ma Bramley with a very determined look in her eye.

This news made Pippin look very glum. "Does that mean I can't see my friends for a whole week?" cried the little pig.

"Not at all!" chuckled Pa Bramley as he came in from his orchard.

"I've made you a gate from the branches of an old apple tree. You can stay in the kitchen on one side of the gate, and your friends can stay on the other. That way you'll be happy,

and your friends won't catch the measles!"

"We will come and see Pippin every day until her spots have disappeared!" cried the children. "Thanks a lot Pa Bramley!"

Plumber Bear's Good Idea

Nanni Bear was having her breakfast early one morning, when she felt a drop of water fall onto her head, and when she looked up at the ceiling, another one splashed onto her nose.

"There must be a leak in the bathroom!" said Nanni as she pushed the teapot into the middle of the table to catch the drips.

"I'll send for Plumber Bear straight away. He'll know what to do!"

When Plumber Bear came at long last, he went straight upstairs. As he walked out of the bathroom he shook his head.

"You need a new bath, and a new wash-basin and a new toilet. Your bath is leaking, your wash-basin is cracked and your toilet is very old-fashioned!"

"No wonder," said Nanni Bear, "they must be at least as old as me. You'd better put in a new bathroom!"

"It will take quite a while," said Plumber Bear. "You never know what I might find!"

So off went Nanni to stay with her sister for a week until the work was done.

When she returned, there was Plumber Bear standing in the garden looking very pleased with himself.

"I know you were fond of your old bathroom so I didn't throw it away," he said grinning and pointing to a corner of the garden. "Here it is!" How Nanni Bear laughed when she saw what Plumber Bear had done!

What Hideous Creatures

One sunny day, a very forgetful professor got down on a grassy bank and began to look at the insects through his magnifying glass.

Now when the professor left for home, he forgot all about his magnifying glass, so straight away all the insects gathered round.

"This is just the thing we need!" and they jumped for joy.

"When the birds fly down to gobble us up, we'll give them a fright for a change!" and so they did.

The birds had never seen such hideous creatures. They took off squawking with fright and never flew down again!

Helga's Toe

Helga the Hippo went for a walk one day. The sky was blue and the sun was warm.

"What a lovely day for a stroll!" bellowed Helga as she thundered along flattening everything in her path.

Now Helga was a particularly huge and heavy hippo, and when she was on the move, everybody got out of her way!

Suddenly as Helga thudded by, a teeny tiny insect stepped on her toe.

"Why can't you pick on someone your own size?" howled Helga as she limped off home!

Huey's Present

Huey the Hairy Caterpillar was looking for a present for his girlfriend.

"Does she like lettuce?" asked a passing ant.

"A lettuce leaf isn't much of a present!" said Huey. "And it's not very romantic!"

"Now you're just being silly," and Huey groaned as he wriggled away.

"How about a fresh spring onion?" suggested a brightly coloured beetle.

"Take her one perfect flower!" a butterfly sighed as she fluttered by.

And straight away, Huey knew that was the right idea.

So he picked a beautiful yellow daisy and crawled off to visit his girlfriend.

"How very romantic!" sighed Huey's girlfriend as she gazed at the flower, then they sat together in the warm sun and ate it!

Rain, Rain, Go Away!

"What a beautiful day," called the youngest grey rabbit as he took a look outside.

"The weather forecast is rain later," said Mrs Grey Rabbit as she hurried to finish her washing.

"Let's go on a picnic," suggested one of the older rabbits, "then we'll be out of Mother's way for a while!"

Although Mrs Rabbit had to admit that this was a good idea, she made all the young rabbits promise to take a rug or cushion in case the grass was damp, and an umbrella or jacket because rain was forecast.

So the little grey rabbits each packed a picnic basket full of their favourite nibbles and set off down the lane.

As they marched along swinging their picnic baskets, they sang at the tops of their voices,

"Rain, rain, go away, Come again another day."

The sun shone brightly all that morning. The little grey rabbits played games in the fields, and at lunchtime they set out their picnic on the grass.

Just as they had finished the last mouthful, the wind blew a big black cloud over their heads and it began to rain.

"Oh dear!" cried the little rabbits all together. "We remembered our picnic baskets, but we forgot our umbrellas and our jackets!"

"Never mind," said one of the rabbits, "we can still keep dry on the way home!" And this is how they did it, as they ran through the raindrops, they sang at the tops of their voices,

"Rain on the green grass,
And rain on the tree,
And rain on the housetop,
But not on me!"

Mrs Grey Rabbit was looking out of the window anxious for her family to return. When she saw them coming down the lane, she had to smile.

"That's one way of keeping dry!" she laughed as she hurried them inside out of the rain.

"Rain, rain, go away,
Come on Mother's washing day!"

Lolli And Pop's New Car

Lolli and Pop took out all their savings from the bank and bought a new car.

They parked it in front of their garden gate and for the rest of the day, Lolli and Pop gazed out of the window admiring it.

"Let's go for a ride," ·said Lolli to Pop next morning. So after breakfast they locked up the house, went down the garden path, Pop got into the driving seat of their shiny new car and turned the key.

"Please start!" said Pop to the little car.

"No" came the reply.

"Please will you take us for a ride?" Lolli asked.

"Won't!" snapped the car.

Would you believe it, every day the same thing happened.

However many times Pop tried to start the car, it simply would not budge.

"It's no good," said Lolli to Pop, "we shall just have to stay at home!"

As time went by, Lolli and Pop's shiny new car began to get dirty parked on the dusty road. The tyres were flat and a careless boy on a bike put a dent in the wing. One of the doors was scratched and the bonnet ' was covered in muddy paw-prints made by next door's cat.

"Our little car is only fit for the scrap yard now," said Lolli to Pop as they leaned over the garden gate.

"What's that I hear?" gasped the little car feeling quite shocked.

"I've been very stupid parked here sulking all this time. I don't want to be sent to the scrap yard!"

So he tried very hard to start his engine. The little car coughed and spluttered, but try as he might, his engine simply would not start!

Lolli and Pop heard their little car and rushed over to help.

Pop threw open the bonnet and tinkered with the engine. Lolli pumped up the tyres then washed and waxed the paintwork.

"I'm afraid you'll have to go to the garage to have that dent in your wing put right," said Pop.

So the two of them jumped into the little car and Pop turned the key.

"Please start!" said Pop to the little car, and the motor began to tick over at once.

"Please will you take us for a ride?" asked Lolli - and off they raced.

Mantu's Little Elephant

Little Mantu lived in a village deep in the jungle where elephants helped the men with their work.

These elephants were so big and strong, they could lift up the heaviest logs with their trunks and toss them high in the air.

Most of the elephants were great show-offs, and Mantu often told them so.

Now, Mantu had an elephant of his very own. His name was Opie. He was just a baby, and Mantu's much loved pet.

"One day when you grow up," Mantu whispered in his Opie's ear, "you'll be the biggest, strongest and bravest in the jungle."

Now the herd of elephants, who had very big ears, heard what Mantu had whispered to Opie.

They began to laugh and stamp their feet and make very rude noises with their long trunks.

"You'll never grow up to be as big as us!" they screeched, and they filled their trunks with water and wet Opie through.

"You're so small, you're nothing at all!" the big elephants chorused rudely.

"We're so tall, we can see over the trees and far away." one sneered.

"In fact, we can see snow sparkling on the tops of the mountains!" and he trumpeted loudly in Opie's ear.

"Is that a fact?" whispered Opie quietly, feeling very small indeed.

"Don't worry!" smiled Mantu throwing both arms round his elephant. "I'm small too, we'll soon grow!"

Then Mantu looked up at the huge elephants with a mischievous glint in his eye. "Although you are very tall and can see over the treetops. We can see what is happening down here in the jungle. In fact we would be the first to see any long, slithering snakes that may be about to coil themselves round your legs!"

"Snakes!" screeched the elephants. "Did you say long, slithering snakes?" and off they thundered in fright.

"Did I say there were snakes?" giggled Mantu. "No, you most definitely did not!" smiled Opie. And Mantu climbed upon his little friends back and went home to the village to tell everyone about the foolish elephants.

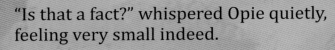

Mr Merry's Brilliant Ideas

It was Mr Merry's birthday and his wife bought him the very latest computer, designed for very clever people only.

"Brilliant!" cried Mr Merry. "I am a very clever person, so I shall sit down at my shiny new computer and begin inventing things straight away.

In the very first hour, Mr Merry invented square wheels.

"No-one has ever thought of square wheels before," chuckled Mr Merry.

"I must be a genius!"

So he fixed them onto Baby Merry's pram. Half-way down the road she got hiccups, so Mr Merry went back to his computer.

It didn't take Mr Merry too long before he came up with another amazing invention - the automatic supermarket trolley.

"No-one will ever _have to push a trolley full of shopping again!" announced Mr Merry - and he was absolutely right.

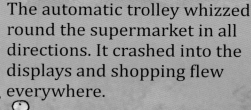

The automatic trolley whizzed round the supermarket in all directions. It crashed into the displays and shopping flew everywhere.

So poor Mr Merry went back to his computer. Soon new ideas came thick and fast. In less time than it takes to count to ten, he had invented blow-up trousers, spring-loaded trainers and an extremely high powered hair-dryer.

Mrs Merry felt that enough was enough. Very quietly she crept over to the computer and pulled out the plug.

"Dear, oh dear!" said Mr Merry puzzled. "I do believe my new computer has broken!"

"Never mind," said Mrs Merry as she sighed with relief. "I think you've invented enough for one day, you can help me with dinner."

"Ace!" cried Mr Merry as he rushed into the kitchen. "I'm brilliant at inventing new dishes. Sit down, dear," he told Mrs Merry, "I'll have the meal cooked in a jiffy!"

So that night, when dinner was ready, Mr and Mrs Merry tucked in to... chocolate fish fingers, striped mashed potatoes, purple peas and a glass of Mr Merry's special fizz-a-lot coke!

A Lick Of Paint

The animals from the toy farm were looking very shabby indeed.

"I once had brown spots," moaned the cow, "look at me now, my paint has peeled off and I'm just plain wood!"

"My feathers used to be all the colours of the rainbow," the turkey sighed.

"I was just as bright as you,' crowed the cockerel, "in fact my feathers were even more colourful!"

"Now stop all that arguing!" scolded the sheep as he looked across at the other animals. "All of us are dull and shabby, every one of us could do with a lick of paint."

"Just a minute," cried one of the toys, "there are some paints in the toy box. Let's find some brushes and brighten up the farm animals."

Several of the toys set to work straight away.

It wasn't as easy as they thought. Some of the farm animals fidgeted and wouldn't stand still. The pony kept tossing his head and two of the lambs knocked over the paint pots.

At last the toys finished, but when they stepped back to admire their work, they got an awful shock.

"You've given me purple spots and green feet!" cried the cow.

"I'm all streaky and striped!" gasped the pony.

"You look a sight!" gobbled the turkey when he saw the cockerel.

"You look even worse!" squawked the cockerel in reply.

"Stop arguing," cried the rag doll.

"This paint will wash off, or so it says on the jar."

So the rag-doll and several of the other toys fetched bowls of soapy water and sponges, and after much rubbing and scrubbing, the farm animals were back to their plain old boring colour once more.

And so they stayed, until Great Uncle Percy came to visit the family.

He took one look in the toy box, spied the farm animals and said in a loud voice. "What a shabby lot, you could do with a lick of paint!"

Now Great Uncle Percy knew a thing or two about animals, he also knew how to paint - as you can see from the results!

Paddy The Park-Keeper

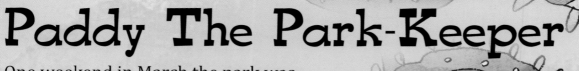

One weekend in March the park was closed for a spring clean and Paddy was very busy.

"I'm pleased this happens just once a year," said Paddy. "The grown-ups don't like the park gates locked and the children hate it!"

So during the next two days Paddy and his helpers went round the park picking up the litter, they weeded the flower-beds and painted all the swings and roundabouts in bright colours.

"Before the park opens tomorrow morning," Paddy told his helpers, "we must be sure to put up notices that say WET PAINT next to the swings and park benches that we've painted."

Then Paddy asked his hardworking helpers if they would like to join him for a cup of tea before they went home.

So they all sat together on a bench in the sunshine and enjoyed a well-earned break. But when they got up to go, every single one of them was covered in wet paint.

"Oh dear," said Paddy, "we should have put the WET PAINT notices out before we sat down!"

The Spooky Old Tree

Mr Badger was strolling through the woods one day when he came across a spooky looking old tree.

"Goodness me!" gasped Mr Badger. "That spooky old tree gave me a real shock."

"Everyone says that!" grumbled a deep voice from down inside the tree's trunk.

"Who said that?" cried Mr Badger glancing around.

"Can't you see?" said the voice. "It's me, the tree!"

Because Mr Badger looked so kind and wise, the tree explained how lonely he was all by himself in the wood.

"I'll admit that I look spooky and scary," the tree told Mr Badger, "but all I need is a bit of company.

Perhaps a few animals could come and live in my trunk, and one or two birds might come and nest in my branches."

"I think I can arrange that," said Mr Badger with a chuckle. "I have a few friends who are looking for a new home - but they can be quite a handful at times, and they make plenty of noise!"

"Bring them along please," begged the tree, "as soon as you can!"

First of all Mr Badger cleared a space round the tree's great trunk.

Then he made new paths that led out of the woods, and edged them with white painted stones.

"I'll put up a light or two before it gets dark, then you'll not look so spooky or scary."

The tree was beginning to enjoy all this attention.

In the next day or so lots of the badger's woodland friends came to visit the tree.

"We would like to make our home in your hollow trunk," said a family of squirrels, "if it's not too much to ask."

"You can have your own flat, right at the top!" laughed the tree, who by now was wearing a big beaming smile.

"Can I have a home too? Twit Twoo!" hooted an owl.

"Please let us dig burrows in your roots!" begged the rabbits.

"Is there room for us in your branches?" cawed the rooks at the tops of their voices.

"I told you some of my friends were a bit noisy." said Mr Badger as he leaned on the tree's trunk.

"I don't mind one little bit," the tree beamed with pleasure," I shall never be lonely again, thanks to you Badger!"

Edwin The Engine

It was snowing quite hard when the engine driver put Edwin the Engine back in his shed after his last journey of the day.

"I think it will snow all night long!" said the engine driver to the guard.

"I've never seen such big snowflakes!" shouted the ticket collector as he looked out of the window.

Very soon the snow was so thick that it covered the station carpark.

"We can't get home tonight," announced the driver.

"Then we'll have to stay here with Edwin!" said the guard and the ticket collector both in the same breath.

So they lit the stove and cooked sausages and beans and made a large pot of coffee.

"It's like camping out!" laughed the guard.

"But much better!" replied the driver and ticket collector as they made themselves comfortable for the night.

As for Edwin the Engine, he thought this was great fun. He enjoyed having company in his train shed. "It's just like an adventure!" he hooted as he dropped off to sleep.

Next morning the snow was so deep, that the railway men couldn't open Edwin's shed doors.

"You'll have to push them open Edwin!" said the driver, so the train drove straight into the doors. "Push Edwin! Push with all your might!"

At last the doors burst open and Edwin chugged slowly out into the sunshine.

What a sight met their eyes! The snow had drifted during the night and had almost covered the station

and most of the town too.

A few brave people had struggled through the snow and were standing on the platform waiting for Edwin.

"We need your help Edwin." said the worried station-master.

"You're the only one that can get through to the farms and houses along the track.

Very soon the baker and grocer were loading boxes of food into Edwin's carriages.

"Can you drop these off to the folks who live by the side of the railway line?" asked the station-master.

"Certainly!" tooted Edwin blowing his whistle loudly.

"Will you take this hay to the cattle and bring back the newborn lambs - so we can find a warm place for them?" went on the worried station-master, who by this time looked like a snowman.

"I'll do my best," replied Edwin as he chugged very slowly out of the station.

It wasn't easy ploughing through the thick snowdrifts, in fact it needed every bit of power in Edwin's engine.

The folks along the track were delighted with the fresh bread and milk and all the food that Edwin had brought them.

"You're a hero!" said one farmer as he loaded his tiny Iambs into Edwin's warm carriage. "My Iambs will be safe now!"

The snow was so deep that it lasted a long, long time. For weeks Edwin took the children to and from school. He brought people fresh bread every morning and big bags of logs for their fires.

When at last the snow melted, everyone felt they should thank Edwin, for looking after them so well.

So on the very first day that the weather was fine, they all gathered at the station and presented Edwin with a brass plaque to go on the front of his engine.

Edwin wears it proudly to this day, and if you should happen to see an engine with a special brass plaque, take a good look - it could be Edwin!

William's Monsters

William had a very vivid imagination and he thought he saw monsters everywhere. Sometimes he would just pretended he did!

When he was walking to school in the morning, he would shout out loudly. "Look at that monster peeping over the fence- he's coming after you!"

"Don't be so silly William!" shouted one of the girls in his class.

She didn't turn round or even bother to look, she just walked on.

"Watch out!" screamed William as he ran after his classmates.

"They're crawling out of cracks in the pavement - there are monsters everywhere!"

But no one ever took the slightest notice of William.

As soon as he returned home William pretended to see monsters in the kitchen and monsters in the hall, he even said he saw them sitting on the stairs.

At bedtime he shouted to his Mum and Dad that there was a monster in the bath and another down the toilet.

"I'm getting very tired of this," said Dad as he turned on the television.

"Don't worry," said Mum with a smile, "He'll grow out of it!"

That night when she went upstairs to tuck William in, she said, "Have you noticed the monster that's crept into your bed?"

William almost jumped out of his skin! After a while his Mum began to laugh.

"You're the little monster William!" she said as she kissed him goodnight!

Warning Lights

Darkness was falling and it was getting late. Lolli and Pop said goodnight to their little car parked by the garden gate, then went inside to get ready for bed.

They hadn't been asleep very long before something woke Lolli up.

"There's a strange light!" whispered Lolli as she shook Pop's arm.

"If I get up and take a look," sighed Pop getting out of bed, "promise we can go back to sleep!"

Now when Pop looked out of the window, he was surprised to see two bright lights flashing outside.

"Perhaps a spaceship has landed in our garden!" gasped Lolli.

"Nonsense!" said Pop. "It's our little car flashing his headlights.

Something must be wrong." As quick as could be, Lolli and Pop ran downstairs and out into the garden in their nightclothes.

"Look!" cried Lolli grabbing Pop's arm. "Our garden fence is on fire!"

"Goodness, gracious me!" cried Pop. "Our little car has tried to warn us by flashing his lights."

"Send for the fire-brigade at once!" Lolli screamed.

"A couple of buckets of water will do nicely!" said Pop calmly. "We don't need to turn out the fire-engine at this time of night."

So Lolli and Pop threw water onto the burning fence and put the fire out straight away.

"By the way," said Lolli looking puzzled, "how did our garden fence get on fire in the first place?"

Pop looked down at his slippers. "I'm afraid it was my fault, Lolli. I had a bonfire and forgot to see that the flames were put out before we went to bed. A spark must have set fire to the fence!"

"It's out now," smiled Lolli, "and there's no harm done."

So before Lolli and Pop went back to bed, they thanked their clever little car and wished him a very goodnight.

A Prince Comes To Visit

In young Mantu's village, deep in the jungle, everyone was getting very excited.

A prince was coming on a very special visit to see the great elephants who lived and worked in the jungle.

"The prince must have heard how big and strong we all are," said the leader of the elephants "and he is going to see for himself!"

"It's a great honour," said Opie the baby elephant to his friend Mantu.

"Yes it is," Mantu replied, "but it will make those elephants more conceited than they already are. If that's possible?"

"Get out of the way you two." the big elephants snapped. "We need to get ready. When the prince comes he will want to meet us. He won't even bother with you!"

So off went the elephants to be dressed up in all their finery.

"I wish I could meet the prince," said Opie to Mantu. "So do I" agreed the little boy.

"We could both get ready, just in case!" and Mantu climbed up on Opie's back and off they went.

Just before the prince was due to arrive, the biggest elephants marched past looking magnificent.

Opie and Mantu hid in the trees to watch.

"It's just like a parade." whispered Opie wide-eyed.

"They're nothing but a bunch of show-offs!" glowered Mantu.

At last the prince arrived and the whole herd of elephants pressed forward to greet him.

"Help!" cried the prince, stepping back in surprise. "Those huge elephants are making the ground tremble!"

If the truth were told - the prince was frightened. "I would like to ride on an elephant," said the prince to his friends, "but these are far too big!"

Then out of the trees stepped Mantu and little Opie.

"Hurrah!" cried the prince, clapping his hands and beaming with joy. "This baby elephant is just the right size for me!" and he climbed up on Opie's back.

You see, no one had told the big elephants that the prince was just a little boy, in fact he was only eight years old!"

72

Always In A Mess

"I do believe that you attract dirt!" said Ashley's dad as he gazed at him in despair.

Ashley had grass stains all over his clothes. He had mud on his face and hair, and goodness knows what he had over his brand new trainers!

"In exactly one hour from now," went on Ashley's dad, "we are going to meet Grandma at the tea-shop for tea. Get cleaned up as fast as you can - and we'll be off straight away."

"No worries!" grinned Ashley as he messed up all the clean towels.

"I can't possibly get dirty in a tea-shop!"

However, Ashley's dad was not so sure.

Now believe it or not, Ashley hadn't been in the tea-shop five minutes, before the lady who serves the tea, tripped over his foot and spilt a whole tray of cakes all over Ashley's dad.

"I'm not in a mess this time. Am I dad?" asked Ashley, still perfectly clean and tidy.

"No, not this time Ashley!" said his dad heaving a big sigh.

Don't Press That Button

Young Mildred Makepeace had a very bad habit - she pressed buttons!

Most of us know which button to press and when to press it.

Unfortunately Mildred did not!

She pressed all the doorbells down the street, then she pressed the button on the fire-alarm- just to see the fire-engine speed past.

"You're a menace!" cried Mildred's mother in despair when her young daughter pressed the wrong button on the washing machine, and the water flooded out all over the kitchen floor.

When people were talking on the telephone, if Mildred walked by, she would press the button and cut the caller off- which was very irritating indeed!

Mildred's mum had lost count of the times she had been stuck in the lift when Mildred pressed the wrong button.

One day in the park, Mildred discovered a button she had never seen before.

"Don't press it Mildred!" yelled her mother.

Without any warning a spurt of ice-cold water hit Mildred in the face and drenched her from top to toe.

Poor Mildred had pressed the button on the drinking. water fountain. Strange to say, after that, Mildred never pressed another button.

Sing 'Happy Birthday'

Scott's little cousin April was very quiet and rather shy.

"What a good little girl," people would say. "She never makes a mess, she doesn't make much noise and she's very tidy. In fact she's perfect!"

April was perfect... until the day that Scott had his birthday party.

All the young guests were sitting around the table, when in came Scott's mother with his birthday cake. There on top were seven brightly lit candles, just waiting to be blown out.

One, two, three, Scott blew them out in one big breath and everyone sang 'Happy Birthday! Scott's little cousin April sang loudest of all (which surprised everyone - because she was so quiet.)

Now as soon as the children stopped singing and began to get on with the games, April started to 'scream, (which was very unlike her - because she was so quiet)

Now the only thing that would stop April screaming was the Happy Birthday song.

The guests sang it over and over again. Scott had to sing when the party was over and all through the next day.

Happy Birthday to you! Happy Birthday to you!

While he sang the song, April was happy and quiet, but as soon as he stopped, April would yell and scream.

What was to be done?

Lucky for everyone, Scott's mother went to the toy store and found a little music box - and what do you think it played?

'Happy Birthday to you' Now Scott's little cousin April is very quiet once more - except when she sings 'Happy Birthday! of course!

Bobbie's Boat

Bobbie the Baker worked hard from morning 'til night.

He had to be at his baker's shop very early indeed.

Bobbie always set his alarm clock to ring at four in the morning. That was the time he started to mix the flour, the water and the yeast, to make the dough, then bake the bread for his customers.

Bobbie loved being a baker and made some of the most delicious bread and tempting cakes you ever tasted.

Although folks came from far and wide to buy his bread, every night when Bobbie closed his shop he always had a few loaves left.

Now Bobbie was a kind-hearted person, and that is why before he went home he filled his baker's basket up with left-over bread, which he fed to the birds who lived on the lake in front of his house.

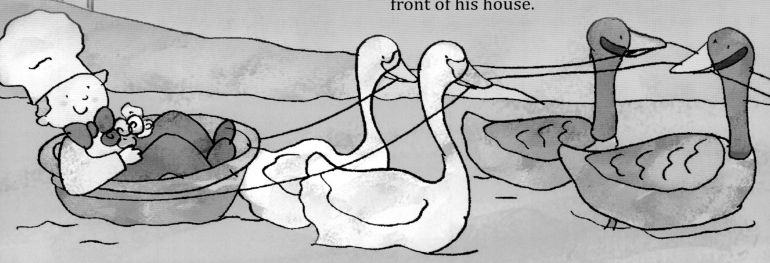

ashore as the boat sank to the bottom of the lake.

"I can't afford to buy another boat," Bobbie told his friends the birds. "I shall never be able to meet my girlfriend again!" and he went inside looking very sad indeed.

So that night the ducks, the geese and the swans held a meeting and very soon came up with an idea.

Next morning the birds were up and about as early as Bobbie.

The swans and the ducks and the geese liked the taste of Bobbie's bread, and gobbled it up eagerly.

"I wish we could do something for Bobbie in return!" hissed a large white swan.

"So do we!" cackled the geese as they landed on the water.

Every single evening when Bobbie had returned home and fed the birds, he would get into his tiny boat and row across the lake to visit his girlfriend, who lived on the opposite side of the lake.

But one night when Bobbie stepped into his boat as usual, he got quite a shock - he was standing up to his ankles in icy cold water.

"There's a hole in my boat!" cried Bobbie in dismay, and he just managed to scramble

"Can you bring your biggest mixing bowl home with you tonight?" asked one of the swans.

"Certainly!" replied Bobbie, who was far too bothered about not seeing his girlfriend to be curious about the bowl.

That night he understood why!

Those clever birds tied long ropes onto the huge mixing bowl and gently towed it across the lake, with Bobbie sitting safely inside.

"At last we can do something for you in return for all the bread you feed us!" chorused the ducks and the geese and the swans.

Seeing The Sights

The zoo-keeper and his wife Norah worked very hard looking after the animals in the zoo.

Sometimes, if every single one of the animals behaved themselves, Norah would think of a special treat that they could all share.

"How would you like to go sightseeing?" Norah asked the animals one day when the zoo was dosed.

"Can we visit a big city and see the sights there?" cried the giraffe who usually kept quiet.

"If it's not too far to walk." said the zoo-keeper in a serious voice (although he was winking at Norah.)

"I'll be alright!" the giraffe butted in. "My legs are so long, I'll be there in a jiffy!"

"How about us?" asked the smaller animals very worried. "We can't walk very far and we don't want to miss our special treat."

Just then a bus drove through the zoo gates and parked in front of the animals.

"This," announced Norah with a wave of her hand, "is a bus especially made for sightseeing." All the animals crowded round. "The smallest of you can sit upstairs, the medium size animals can sit downstairs, and the larger animals can sit upstairs and downstairs at the same time!"

It took the animals quite a while to fit into the bus, but at last they were ready for off.

"I think we should go sightseeing more often!" smiled the zoo-keeper.

"I agree!" laughed his wife Norah.

Snowdrop Tricks Mr Magic

Mr Magic had a pet rabbit called Snowdrop who helped him with his tricks on stage.

The little white rabbit liked being part of Mr Magic's act, especially when he pulled him out of his top-hat

"I'm going to play a trick on Mr Magic for a change," giggled Snowdrop, "it will be great fun!"

So he set to work. First he pulled a long string of coloured flags from Mr Magic's pocket, then he plucked a whole pack of cards from behind his ears.

"You'll have to do better than that!" laughed Mr Magic as he produced a bunch of flowers from his sleeve. "I know every trick there is!"

Next day Snowdrop got a letter from his brother, asking if he might come and stay for a while.

"Please tell your brother to come over right away" said Mr Magic kindly. "You never know, he might like to help us in our act"

"I'm sure he'd love that," said Snowdrop with a little secret grin.

When Snowdrop's brother arrived the next day, Mr Magic was already on stage in the middle of his act

When he came to the very last trick, Mr Magic waved his wand and pulled Snowdrop out of his top-hat as usual.

The audience gasped, then began to clap and cheer - it wasn't Snowdrop, but there instead was a soft fluffy black rabbit. Poor Mr Magic almost dropped him in surprise.

"That's my brother!" whispered Snowdrop giggling behind the curtain.

"I've tricked you at last!" and Mr Magic had to agree.

Teddy's Invitation

One morning an important envelope arrived for Teddy in the post.

"It isn't my birthday for months," said Teddy puzzled, "although it looks just like a birthday card."

"I can guess what it is!" cried one of the smaller dolls. "It's an invitation. Open it up and tell us who it's from!"

So Teddy did just that. "It's a wedding invitation," gasped Teddy looking shocked, "I've never been to a wedding before."

It was from the bride-doll who was getting married the following Saturday, and she wanted Teddy to come to the wedding.

"Whatever shall I wear?" Teddy asked the other toys. "Does anyone know?"

"You must look very smart," said the soldier-doll. "Try my uniform on for size."

Now when Teddy tried it on, all the toys began to laugh.

"It's a little on the small side," whispered the toy rabbit shyly.

"I think you ought to go down to the costume shop and hire a best suit."

So off went Teddy on the rabbit's advice.

The costume shop was full of very smart clothes. "Better make a start!" said Teddy out loud as he began to try the suits on.

The first one had a coat with tails which made Teddy trip up.

The second was too small. The trousers were too short, the waistcoat was so tight the buttons popped off, and the sleeves of the jacket only reached Teddy's elbows.

"How about a top-hat?" the man in the shop asked Teddy. "You should always wear a top-hat at a wedding!"

Teddy tried them all. What a shock he got when he saw himself in the mirror.

"We don't seem to have anything in your size" said the man in the shop as he rolled up his tape measure.

Sadly Teddy left the shop, but when he reached home he was surprised to see the bride-doll standing in his garden.

"I'm afraid I can't find anything to wear at your wedding!" said Teddy looking glum.

The bride-doll stared at Teddy in surprise. "Just come as yourself.

You look just perfect as you are!" and she gave Teddy a kiss and a great big hug.

The Moon, A Balloon And A Spoon

This is a very strange story about the moon, a balloon and a spoon- but who's to say it isn't true?

It happened late one night when everybody had gone to bed. All the children in the houses had been fast asleep for hours, and all the grown-ups too. Only the cats that sat on the rooftops were wide awake in the moonlight.

Suddenly there came a noise like thunder perhaps, or a jet plane maybe, or the roaring, rushing sound of a hurricane. No-one could really say for sure.

All at once everyone was out of bed opening their windows and looking up into the sky.

There it was again, and again, and again. The noise was so loud that it knocked off some of the chimney pots and sent them rolling down the roofs.

"What is it?" the people in the houses cried with fright.

A ginger cat who' had been sitting on the roof seemed to know the answer.

"It's the Moon!" he purred, looking very aloof. "The Moon has a bad cold and he keeps on sneezing!" and the ginger cat strolled off to find a quieter rooftop.

Sure enough when the people looked up into the sky, they could see that the Moon had a dreadful cold - red nose and all!

The stars were scattered across the sky, for they found it very difficult to hang on when the Moon was sneezing so hard.

All through that night the Moon sneezed and sneezed. No-one got a wink of sleep and everyone felt very tired and grumpy next morning.

"What are we going to do?" neighbours asked one another- but nobody had the least idea.

"How long does a bad cold usually last?" someone asked the chemist in the shop down the street.

"At least a week," he said gravely, "and in some cases up to a fortnight!"

Everybody groaned. No sleep for a fortnight - it was unthinkable! "What the Moon really needs is a bottle of my best cold medicine," the chemist went on, "that will stop him sneezing in a jiffy."

"This all sounds very silly indeed," said a lady who lived in one of the houses. "How on earth can we give medicine to the Moon?"

"Somebody could float up there in a balloon," said one little boy "they do it all the time in nursery rhymes and fairy stories!"

"That sounds like a very good idea to me," a man spoke up, "I have a hot-air balloon and would gladly help the Moon's bad cold!"

First the medicine had to be mixed. The chemist found everything he needed and put all the ingredients into a great big bowl. He had a giant bottle in his shop window so he carefully poured the cold mixture into that.

"So far so good," smiled the chemist looking very pleased with himself.

"We shall need a giant spoon!" piped up the little boy (whose idea it was in the first place).

"I've just the thing." cried the baker. "I use it to stir my cakes at Christmas time - I've such a lot to make!" So straight away he ran to his shop to fetch the giant spoon.

The man who owned the hot-air balloon started getting things ready.

The little boy (whose idea it was in the first place), was going up in the basket to give the Moon the medicine.

By the time darkness fell and the Moon appeared in the sky, everything was ready.

You could hear that the Moon's cold was no better, in fact he sounded much worse. Even the clouds were being blown all over the place.

"Soon we shall be sneezing instead of twinkling." some of the stars grumbled loudly.

At long last the man in the hot air balloon and the little boy, (whose idea it was in the first place), reached the Moon.

Very, very carefully the little boy gave the Moon the cold medicine from the giant spoon.

"Is it alright to take the whole bottle?" asked the Moon wheezing and sneezing.

"Perfectly alright," the little boy replied, "it says so on the label!"

The cold medicine worked wonders. In next to no time the Moon recovered and all was peace and quiet.

Everyone in the houses had a good night's sleep, for there was nothing to disturb their slumbers and the cats walked along the rooftops as usual and gazed up at the Moon, who was fast asleep too!

Father Bear Does The Washing Up

Father Bear hated washing up. The cups and saucers weren't too bad, but he simply hated the dirty, greasy pans.

Now in the Bear's house, everyone took turns to wash up, and tonight, was Father Bear's turn.

"What are we having for supper tonight dear?" asked Father Bear from behind his newspaper.

"Omelette with salad," replied Mother Bear. "I'm just going to fetch the pan now!"

''Wonderful," chuckled Father Bear to himself, "that means only one little pan for me to wash up!"

How wrong he was! Mother Bear had only just begun to cook the omelette, when Baby Bear cried to be lifted out of his high chair, and when Mother returned the omelette was burnt and stuck to the pan.

"Oh dear," said Mother Bear, "what a shame, we'll have to have soup instead!"

So she filled a huge pan with thick, tasty soup and left it to simmer on the stove.

Just at that moment there was a telephone call for Mrs Bear, and when she came back the soup had boiled over, all down the sides of the pan.

Suddenly there came a knock at the door. "I'll answer it," cried Father Bear, "while you look after the spaghetti!"

Surprise, surprise, it was the delivery bear with a pile of pizzas!

"Oh dear," said Mother Bear, "I had quite forgotten I'd ordered pizza for supper. What a shame, I needn't have messed up all those pans!"

I think Father Bear will be washing up for quite a while, don't you.

"Oh dear," said Mother Bear, "what a shame, we'll have to have sausages!"

As soon as the sausages were sizzling and spitting in the frying pan, Brenda Bear needed a button stitching on her blouse, and when Mother Bear returned the frying pan was alight and the sausages were burnt to a cinder.

"Oh dear," said Mother Bear, "what a shame, we'll have to have spaghetti!"

So she took down her biggest pan, filled it full of boiling water and tossed in the spaghetti.

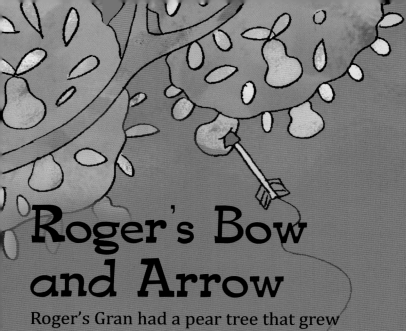

Roger's Bow and Arrow

Roger's Gran had a pear tree that grew right alongside the wall of her house.

Sometimes when Roger stayed with his Gran, if the fruit was ready, he would lean out of the bedroom window and pick a juicy, ripe pear.

"Don't forget," said Roger every autumn, "Grans are not supposed to climb ladders, it's far too dangerous. I will pick the pears for you!"

"Very well!" said Gran with a sigh, (because she loved climbing ladders), but she said

she wouldn't, and Grans always keep their promises!

"Why do the biggest and best pears grow on the end of the branches where no one can reach them?" Gran asked Roger as they were picking the fruit.

"I can't reach them from the ladder or from the bedroom window," said Roger looking puzzled, "but I know how I can!" and he ran indoors.

"What on earth are you going to shoot with that bow and arrow?" Gran gasped. "Not me, I hope!" and she laughed.

Now Roger had tied a string to each of his arrows - which had little suckers in the end instead of sharp tips.

Every time he hit a pear, Roger gave the string a quick tug, and the fruit fell into Gran's outstretched apron.

"Right on target!" cried Roger
"Right on!" laughed his Gran.

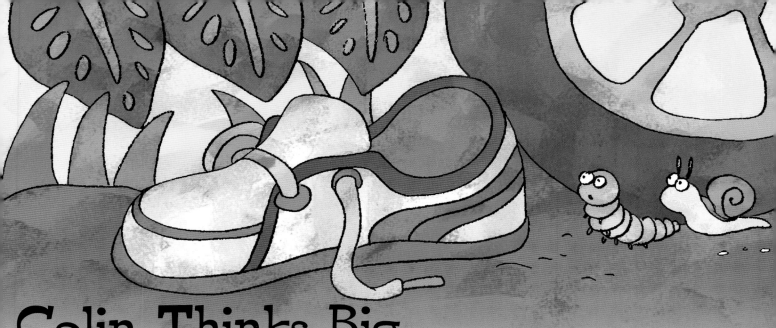

Colin Thinks Big

Colin Caterpillar and Sylvia Snail were crawling along the garden wall one sunny morning.

"Isn't the world big!" remarked Colin as he gazed around.

"It's huge, it's gigantic, it's enormous, it's vast!" agreed Sylvia, who thought a lot about such things inside that shell of hers.

"It makes me feel so very small," Colin went on.

"But I know a way to change all that!" said Sylvia wisely.

So the two of them spent the rest of that morning collecting the teeniest, weeniest, tiniest things they could find.

Colin collected a crumb, a pea, a shell and a petal. Very soon he had found a feather, a peanut, a button and a berry.

Sylvia brought back a drawing pin, a paper clip, a pen nib, a pin and a needle.

"Look! You're almost a giant Colin!" and off she crawled.

"How small these things are," chuckled Colin, "and look how big I am!"

Mr Wolf's Speed-boat

The three little pigs loved to spend a day by the river just messing about in their small boats.

On fine mornings they would get up early, and if there was no sign of rain, the three pigs would pack a picnic and set off for the river where their boats were moored.

One little pig had a blue and yellow rowing boat, one had a canoe, and the other little pig had a raft made from bits and bobs he'd collected.

Now some times wicked Mr Wolf would creep up behind them. At first the three little pigs thought he was after their picnic. But they soon realised that he wanted to eat them, not their food!

But try as he might, Mr Wolf simply couldn't catch the three little pigs, for as soon as they knew he was around, they jumped into their small boats and paddled into the middle of the river where they knew they would be safe.

That is until one dreadful day, when wicked Mr Wolf went out and bought a boat of his own.

The three little pigs were paddling their small boats in the middle of the river as usual, when suddenly, out of the reeds zoomed Mr Wolf in a bright red speed-boat!

That bad Mr Wolf raced towards the three little pigs as fast as he could. He sped round and round them churning the water into huge waves. It wasn't long before the small boats were overturned and the three little pigs were tipped into the water.

"Help! Help! Help!" yelled the poor pigs as they bobbed up and down very wet and frightened. But Mr Wolf sped off down the river towards the sea laughing all the way.

As Mr Wolf whizzed through the water, he passed so close to the water-vole's house-boat, that some of the smaller members of the family fell overboard into the river.

This made Mr Wolf laugh even louder. He was having great fun!

Very soon Mr Wolf reached the end of the river. Here were lots of boats going about their business, sailing on the open sea or coming in and out of the harbour.

Without even stopping to think, Mr Wolf drove his speed-boat as fast as he could right through the middle of them. He overturned two yachts and wrecked a motor-boat.

Because of Mr Wolf, a tug almost crashed into a trawler and all the smaller boats had to make for the safety of the harbour.

All of a sudden Mr Wolf's speed-boat stopped. Although he tried with all his

might, the wicked wolf could not re-start the engine and his boat began to drift out to sea.

"Help somebody, help!" screamed Mr Wolf "I've stopped! I'm all alone! I can't swim and I'm frightened!"

But nobody heard Mr Wolf. Everyone was far too busy trying to sort out the damage he had caused to the boats in the harbour.

Soon it began to grow dark. No-one remembered Mr Wolf. So he sat alone in his speed-boat until it was dawn, the tide came in and gently washed Mr Wolf back into the harbour.

"I couldn't start my engine!" sobbed Mr Wolf very stiff and cold.

"I'm not surprised," shouted one of the fishermen on board a trawler. "You must have run out of petrol!"

How silly Mr Wolf looked.

When the three pigs heard about his unfortunate adventure, they laughed until they cried.

"Serves him right!" giggled one little pig.

"Lucky we were wearing life jackets when he overturned our boats!" said another.

"I bet the wicked wolf will never spoil our days out on the river again!" and the three little pigs went on laughing!

Baby Hedgehog Makes The Dinner

Mrs Hedgehog and her family were all outside working in the garden.

Baby Hedgehog could see how busy they were as he stood by the kitchen door.

Carefully he turned every page. "These recipes all look delicious."

But then Baby Hedgehog remembered that he couldn't read, so he put the cookery book back on the shelf.

'I can make toast and cheese sandwiches," said Baby Hedgehog as he sat at the table, "but they're a bit boring!"

So he jumped down from his stool and looked inside all the kitchen cupboards to see what he could find.

Two of the young hedgehogs were digging, two more were hoeing, and the rest were planting vegetable seeds.

"There's such a lot of gardening to be done." said Baby Hedgehog.

"Everybody will be very hungry when dinner time comes," and as he walked back into the kitchen, he had a wonderful idea. "I shall make the dinner and surprise everybody!"

So straight away Baby Hedgehog took down his mother's cookery book to help him decide what to make for dinner.

Then he discovered some jelly beans and half a packet of peanuts.

"They'll do for decoration with a blob of cream on top - finished at last!"

Baby Hedgehog opened the kitchen drawer, took out a spoon and tried a little sample from the bowl, then he tried a bit more until he began to feel quite sick.

And so it was that at dinner time, when Mrs Hedgehog and all the other little hedgehogs

Very soon he came across lots of things that he knew the little hedgehogs liked to eat.

"I shall mix them all together in one big bowl, and then everybody will have a lovely dinner!"

First Baby Hedgehog put in a packet of chocolate biscuits, a tub of vanilla ice-cream and a jug of custard.

Next, he found some peaches in a tin. "They will do nicely!" said the little hedgehog, very pleased with himself.

"We all love spaghetti with some tomato sauce." So that went into the bowl too.

came in feeling very hungry, they found Baby Hedgehog sitting at the table looking rather green.

"I think I'd better make beans on toast for all of us." said Mrs Hedgehog as she looked inside the mixing bowl.

"Nothing for me thank you!" said Baby Hedgehog very quietly.

Tilly's Grin

Baby Tilly was very special. Her Mum and Dad told her so at least twenty times day.

"You're so special!" cooed her Mum.

"My little precious!" smiled her Dad as he tickled Tilly under her chin.

"Let's take her photo!" cried Mum and Dad together.

Now Tilly's photo had been taken every day since she was born, and on every single one of them she was frowning.

"Give us a grin!" pleaded her Dad.

"Just one little smile!" begged her Mum.

But Tilly just frowned and kept on frowning - until one glorious day.

Tilly woke up and a huge beaming smile spread right across her face.

She opened her mouth and gave a great big grin, and there in the middle were two new front teeth!

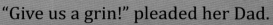

A String Of Beads

Dolly, Molly and Holly liked to thread beads on a string. They had boxes and jars filled with pretty coloured beads of every shape and size and colour.

Sometimes the girls made necklaces, sometimes they made bracelets, and often they would just thread their beads on a long string.

Dolly, Molly and Holly were always careful to pick up the beads they had dropped on the floor, just in case they got sucked into Mum's vacuum cleaner and were lost for ever.

One day the three girls decided that they would thread the longest string of beads in the world. They set to work and by bedtime had made a necklace that stretched all round the table, and then some!

"Does anyone mind if I borrow this piece of string?" asked Dad as he got up from his chair.

"Be careful!" shrieked all three girls. Too late! Dad pulled the string and hundreds of beads were scattered all over the floor. Dad took one step and went flying too.

So poor Dolly, Molly and Holly had to start threading their beads all over again!

The Little Lost Hedgehog

Mrs Hedgehog had such a large family that she had to wash lots of clothes everyday.

When the weather was warm and breezy, all ten young hedgehogs lent a hand, and the washing was done in next to no time.

"Today is perfect for washing our clothes," said Mrs Hedgehog, as she gave everyone a job. "Two of you scrub the clothes, two of you rinse off the soap suds, two of you wring them dry, two of you hang them on the line,

and two tiny ones hand me the pegs!" Very soon all the dirty clothes were clean and bright and hanging on the clothes line in the sun.

"We all deserve a rest," smiled Mrs Hedgehog. So she sat down on the grassy bank near the clothesline, took off her hat and put it down by her side. All her little hedgehogs sat beside her with glasses of cool lemonade and buttery biscuits.

"How lucky I am," thought Mrs Hedgehog, "to have such helpful children." All of a sudden she gave a squeal. "There are only nine of you!

Where is Baby Hedgehog?" The young hedgehogs put down their lemonade and biscuits and began to search at once. They looked everywhere, in the house, in the garden, in the meadow, in the wood, they even looked in the empty clothes baskets.

"Baby Hedgehog can't have disappeared," cried Mrs Hedgehog, very worried. "He was sitting right next to me on this grassy bank eating his buttery biscuit!"

The rest of that day all the hedgehogs searched long and hard. The sun began to set behind the hill and soon it would be dark.

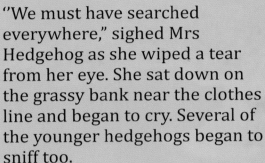

"We must have searched everywhere," sighed Mrs Hedgehog as she wiped a tear from her eye. She sat down on the grassy bank near the clothes line and began to cry. Several of the younger hedgehogs began to sniff too.

Poor Mrs Hedgehog bent over to pick up her hat that she had left there since the morning and what do you think she saw?

Baby Hedgehog fast asleep! He must have crawled under his mother' hat and fallen asleep in the sun.

How the young hedgehogs cheered, they were so happy to find Baby Hedgehog. They made such a noise that their woodland friends nearby came out to join in the celebrations.

The Pink Elephant's Party

When Pink Elephant moved to Toy Town she was rather worried. "I hope I shall make new friends quickly," she said, as she unlocked the door to her new home.

At first Pink Elephant was busy settling in. She moved the furniture around until everything was exactly in the right place. Then, she put up brand new curtains, hung her favourite paintings on the walls, and filled all her vases with bunches of summer flowers.

"How lovely everything looks!" sighed Pink Elephant happily, and she sat down to admire her new home.

"It's very quiet in Toy Town," thought Pink Elephant, as she gazed out of the window into the empty street.

"I have an idea," she cried jumping up. "I'll give a party and invite everybody in the street. That way I will soon make friends."

So, there and then, Pink Elephant wrote out a huge pile of party invitations for the next afternoon. Then she ran up and down the street popping an envelope through every letter box.

The rest of the day Pink Elephant tidied her front garden. She mowed the lawn and swept the path.

She polished the knocker on the front door and put the numbers back on the gate because they had fallen off.

Next morning, Pink Elephant got up very early and baked all kinds of lovely things to eat. After lunch, she decorated the house with balloons and coloured streamers. Last of all, she put on her party dress and. then waited for her guests to arrive.

Pink Elephant waited and waited, but no-one came. She waited until it was past tea-time, but not one single guest arrived.

At last she opened her front door and walked down the garden path to the gate. What a surprise the Pink Elephant got! There were crowds of toys walking past with armfuls of presents and cards.

"Where are you all going?" shouted Pink Elephant, as they walked by.

"To Pink Elephant's party!" cried a furry rabbit as he waved the invitation in the air.

"But the party is here, at my house!" said Pink Elephant. "Why are you all walking past?"

"You live at Number 31," the rabbit answered, "and the invitation says Number 13."

"Oh dear!" gasped Pink Elephant. "I must have put the numbers back on my gate the wrong way round!"

How the toys laughed. They all crowded into Number 13. Pink Elephant gave a wonderful party and made lots of new friends.

Ben's New Seat

Once upon a time, a grizzly bear called Ben made himself a seat.

"I'm rather lonely by myself in the forest," said Ben. "I shall sit here on my seat and see who passes by."

Very soon, along came a grey rabbit who hopped up onto Ben's knee. Then a squirrel jumped down from a branch overhead.

Two racoons who were scampering by, stopped when they saw Ben's seat, then jumped up on either side of him.

"Is there room for us?" asked a red fox and a stoat.

"And us?" squeaked a family of mice.

"It's a bit of a squeeze," shouted Ben. So everyone moved in tight and chattered together all afternoon.

They made such a noise that a tiny bluebird flew across to join in the fun. "Can I perch on your seat please?" the tiny bird asked Ben as he fluttered down.

Sadly, that was too much for Ben's new seat. It creaked and groaned and cracked. One by one the wooden legs snapped and everyone fell onto the ground laughing and giggling.

"Tomorrow I shall make a brand new seat, big enough for all my new friends," chuckled grizzly bear Ben, happily.

Three Jolly Fishermen

Once upon a time three jolly fishermen went to sea in a boat with a bright green sail.

The three jolly fishermen loved music and as they fished they sang.

When the sea was calm and still, they sang quiet lullabies. When the boat bobbed up and down on the waves they sang jolly songs together. But when stormy winds blew and great waves crashed over their tiny boat, they sang opera as loud as they could.

Everyday the three jolly fisherman went out in their boat with the bright green sail, but they never ever caught a fish.

And this is the reason why!

The three jolly fisherman made such a noise that all the fish could hear them. As soon as they began to sing, every fish in the bay would gather under the boat with the bright green sail and sing along. The lobsters and crabs, all the fish and huge whales, joined a choir under the sea.

They were so busy singing together and learning new songs, they never ever got caught. And so none of them ended up on a plate for tea!

The Little Green Tractor

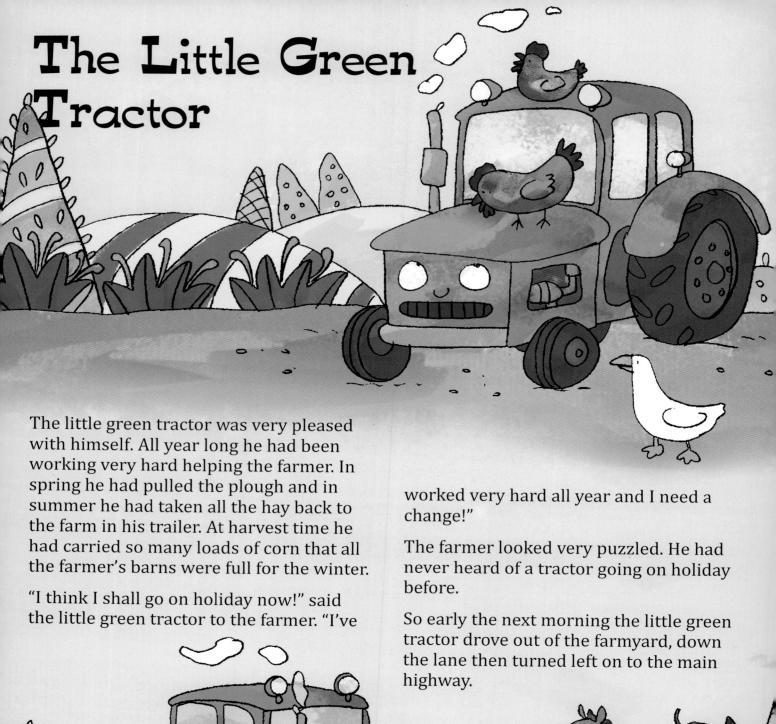

The little green tractor was very pleased with himself. All year long he had been working very hard helping the farmer. In spring he had pulled the plough and in summer he had taken all the hay back to the farm in his trailer. At harvest time he had carried so many loads of corn that all the farmer's barns were full for the winter.

"I think I shall go on holiday now!" said the little green tractor to the farmer. "I've worked very hard all year and I need a change!"

The farmer looked very puzzled. He had never heard of a tractor going on holiday before.

So early the next morning the little green tractor drove out of the farmyard, down the lane then turned left on to the main highway.

At first the road was quiet and the little green tractor chugged along happily. A few cars and vans drove past him and one or two lorry drivers waved as they went by.

On and on went the little green tractor until he came to a busy town.

Here the road was filled with traffic and everyone was travelling very fast.

All of a sudden the cars, buses and trucks screeched to a halt at the traffic lights. But the little green tractor just carried on. (He had never seen a red light before, and didn't know he must stop!)

What a noise the other traffic made. They blew their horns so loudly at the little green tractor that he almost crashed.

As soon as he could, the frightened little green tractor turned off the main road into a garage and came to a stop.

"How I wish I was back home on the farm," said the little green tractor. "Now I shall never get home!"

As soon as the garage owner saw the little green tractor he was puzzled. "What on earth are you doing here?" he asked. "Have you lost your way?"

The little green tractor didn't know what to say.

"Our driver is taking a tanker full of fuel to your farm in five minutes. He'll give you a tow."

So that is how the little green tractor got safely back to the farm.

That night the farmer filled the little green tractor up with fuel and checked his engine. Then he gave the paintwork a polish until it shone.

Nothing was said about tractors going on holiday ever again!

The Bucket With A Hole

A small girl called Jane spent a week by the sea. She had a wonderful time. The weather was fine and the sea was warm and clear. Jane loved to carry water from the sea in her bright red bucket and then pour it into a deep hole she made with her spade. It was great fun!

On the very last day of her holiday, Jane found a hole in her bucket, then she noticed that the handle was loose.

"My bucket's no good any more!" said Jane sadly as she left it on the beach and went home.

"That's the end of me," said the bright red bucket as he lay forgotten on the sand.

A crab came over to try and cheer him up. "Something is bound to turn up," said the crab kindly, but still the bucket felt very miserable.

After a few days, a little boy came running across the beach. He saw the bright red bucket, but didn't mind that it had a hole and a broken handle. He shouted, "You're just what I need!" and picked up the bucket straight away.

The bucket and the little boy stayed together all summer long and when the little boy went home he took the bucket with him!

Archie Goes Visiting

Archie, the polar bear, lived in the Arctic, quite close to the North - Pole. He didn't mind the freezing cold or the bitter winds at all because he had a coat of thick white fur to keep him warm. Archie could go for a swim in the ice-cold sea, then sit down on the ice and he didn't even shiver.

"I love living in the Arctic," said Archie, "except for one thing!"

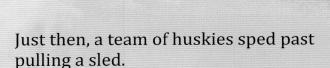

"What's that then?" asked a Walrus. who had just scrambled up onto the ice.

"I have such a long way to walk to visit my polar bear friends!" said Archie with a sigh.

"How about going by air?" asked the Walrus, as he pointed to an aircraft that had just landed on the ice.

"I'm far too big to fit into one of those!" the polar bear laughed.

"It would never take off!"

Just then, a team of huskies sped past pulling a sled.

"Stop a minute!" yelled Archie, as he ran after them. "Can you give me a lift?" but the dogs just stuck out their tongues and ran even faster.

"I suppose I shall have to walk all the way as usual," sighed Archie, as he set off across the ice to visit his friends.

All of a sudden, something whizzed past him and pulled up at the explorers' camp over the hill.

"A snow mobile!" yelled Archie.

"That's just what I need!"

The explorers were quite surprised when a polar bear knocked at their door. Archie asked in such a polite voice to borrow their snow mobile, they just couldn't refuse.

So if you ever visit the frozen lands quite close to the North Pole, and if you should happen to spot a polar bear whizzing across the ice on a snow mobile, it's likely to be Archie visiting his friends!

The Flying Mail

Everyone loves to hear the postman knocking at the door, especially when he has a letter for you.

Bertie Badger was the woodland postman. He had to walk a very long way to deliver his letters to houses all over the wood.

One day as he was sitting on a log having a rest and a cup of tea, a pigeon flew down to join him.

"Would you like some help?" he cooed.

Postman Badger laughed and gave the pigeon some of his sandwich.

"You're a bit too small to be a postman."

Off flew the pigeon and very soon came back with some of his friends. When they saw Bertie Badger's sack they set to work straight away.

The smaller birds sorted the mail while the bigger birds carried the parcels between them.

Postman Badger watched in amazement. The birds came everyday to help deliver the mail on time and Postman Badger made extra sandwiches for them all - just to say thank you.

Texas Grandpa's Jeep

One day Texas Grandpa noticed that his Jeep had a flat front tyre. His grandson Pete went to the garage and pumped it up with the air hose.

Texas Grandpa talked so much that Pete forgot to switch off the hose. Now look at the tyre!

"Grandson Pete," shouted Texas Grandpa. "Pump up the other three!"

Now look at the jeep!

"That's just dandy!" yelled Texas Grandpa as he threw his hat high in the air.

"I've always wanted big wheels!"

Ordinary Street

Down Ordinary Street lived Mr Black. Mrs Grey lived just next door. Mr Brown lived on the other side, but the house next door to him was empty. No-one had lived there for a long time and the house had nothing inside.

One day Mrs White came to buy the house. "Oh dear! I couldn't live here!" she cried. "It's dusty and full of cobwebs." So she went away.

Next Mr Green came to look at the house. "The garden is far too small. There is no room for all my plants!" And he marched off down the street.

The following day Mrs Yellow arrived to look inside. "My goodness," she gasped, "it's far too dark. I need sunshine in every room!" And she drove off in her open car.

Now one dark day, when Ordinary Street was wet with rain, a truck full of noisy children came screeching round the corner.

Suddenly the rain clouds blew away, a patch of blue appeared in the sky and the sun shone brightly.

"We are the Rainbows," called the family to Mr Black, Mrs Grey and Mr Brown who were watching from their front doors.

"What a wonderful house!" gasped Mr and Mrs Rainbow and all the Rainbow children. I think we shall stay here for ever." And they did!

They painted the house in bright colours and filled the garden with beautiful flowers.

"I think," said Mr Black to Mr Grey. "we ought to do the same."

"I agree," nodded Mr Brown. So they started at once.

Soon the street looked so different that it didn't seem ordinary any more.

"Let's call it Bright Street." So they changed the name right away!

Mr Maggs And Monty

Little Mr Maggs had a big dog named Monty who loved to go for very long walks. Monty's legs were so long that little Mr Maggs had to run to keep up with him.

Every morning after breakfast, Monty would wait by the front door for little Mr Maggs to put on his hat and coat and take him out again.

They would walk all afternoon and come back home just in time for tea. Then after a quick snooze in front of the fire, Monty was ready to go out again.

Sometimes it was almost dark when they returned. Then little Mr Maggs would hang up Monty's lead and go straight to bed, quite tired out.

One morning after breakfast Monty went to the back door as usual, waiting to go for a walk. But little Mr Maggs put on his hat and coat and went out leaving Monty at home.

Little Mr Maggs hurried to the shops and came back with a mysterious parcel.

After lunch as usual, little Mr Maggs put on his hat and coat and put Monty's lead on him.

Soon they were both whizzing along. Monty ran faster and faster, but still Mr Maggs kept up. Monty couldn't understand why!

At last poor Monty had to stop for a rest and when he looked round, he saw that little Mr Maggs was wearing ROLLER SKATES!

That is what was in the mysterious parcel.

The Big Blue Balloon

Tom and Peter bought two big balloons. Tom's balloon was red and Peter's balloon was blue.

The next day as Tom was looking out of his bedroom window, he saw a big blue balloon.

"That must be Peter!" laughed naughty Tom. "I'll burst his big blue balloon!" So, very quietly, Tom opened the window, and using a sharp pin he burst the big blue balloon. It went off with a very loud bang.

That made Tom laugh even more. Straight away there was a loud knocking on Tom's door. He ran downstairs at once, and from behind the front door a very big voice boomed, "Who burst my big blue balloon?"

Now Tom had some quick thinking to do!

What A Strange House!

"What a lovely morning," said Lottie, as she opened the front door.

"I think I shall go for a ride on my bike." So she ran upstairs to find her shorts.

When she opened the shed door; Lottie got quite a surprise.

"Someone has been very busy in here!" she cried, then ran outside to find her grandad.

Two blackbirds had built a nest in the basket on the front of her bike.

"No more bike rides for you for a while!" chuckled Grandad.

Later she called at the farm on the hill and she saw a duck sitting on six eggs. Lottie could hardly believe her eyes, the nest was on the farmer's old tractor seat!

"What a strange house for blackbirds," giggled Lottie. 'I'll go for a walk and see what else I can find."

When Lottie called at the cottage down the lane, she found that two swallows had built a nest in the front porch. Everyone would have to use the back door for a few weeks.

Next she met her friend from school who had just found a robin's nest in a plant· pot.

Then a lady called her over to see some mice nesting in a garden chair.

"What strange houses I've seen today!" said Lottie as she ran past the mill.

"Come in and see our new kittens, they've made their home in a barrel," shouted the miller's wife.

Lottie rushed inside and bent down to find six tiny kittens fast asleep in an old flour barrel.

"I have a surprise for you Lottie," whispered the miller's wife in her ear. "Your grandad has asked you to choose two kittens for your very own, and take them back home today!"

How carefully Lottie walked back home, with her two kittens tucked up in a shopping basket.

Her grandad was smiling as he opened the back door. "Now where are you going to keep those Lottie?"

As soon as she put the basket on the floor, both kittens jumped out and ran straight into Lottie's dolls' house.

"What a strange house for two kittens," laughed Lottie. "Welcome to your new home!"

As for the kittens, they were already fast asleep.

The Lonely Monkey

Far away across a bright blue ocean was a tiny desert island.

Everyday the sun shone down on the sandy beach and warmed the clear waters around the shore.

In the middle of this island grew tall palm trees full of coconuts and banana plants loaded with bunches of ripe bananas.

And who do you think lived in this wonderful place? Just one little brown monkey with a curly tail.

"I'm so lonely, I wish I had a friend!" said the monkey out loud as he sat on the beach. But he knew there was no-one to hear him.

A brilliant coloured fish swimming by, stuck his head out of the water. "Follow me and swim to the next island. It's full of little brown monkeys with curly tails just like you!"

"But I can't swim," cried the monkey. "Please fish, will you teach me how?"

"Certainly!" replied the fish.

"Just walk into the water and do as I say."

So the little brown monkey walked slowly into the sea.

"Now take your feet off the bottom and move your arms," cried the fish.

"Oh dear!" shrieked the monkey. "I don't like this one bit!

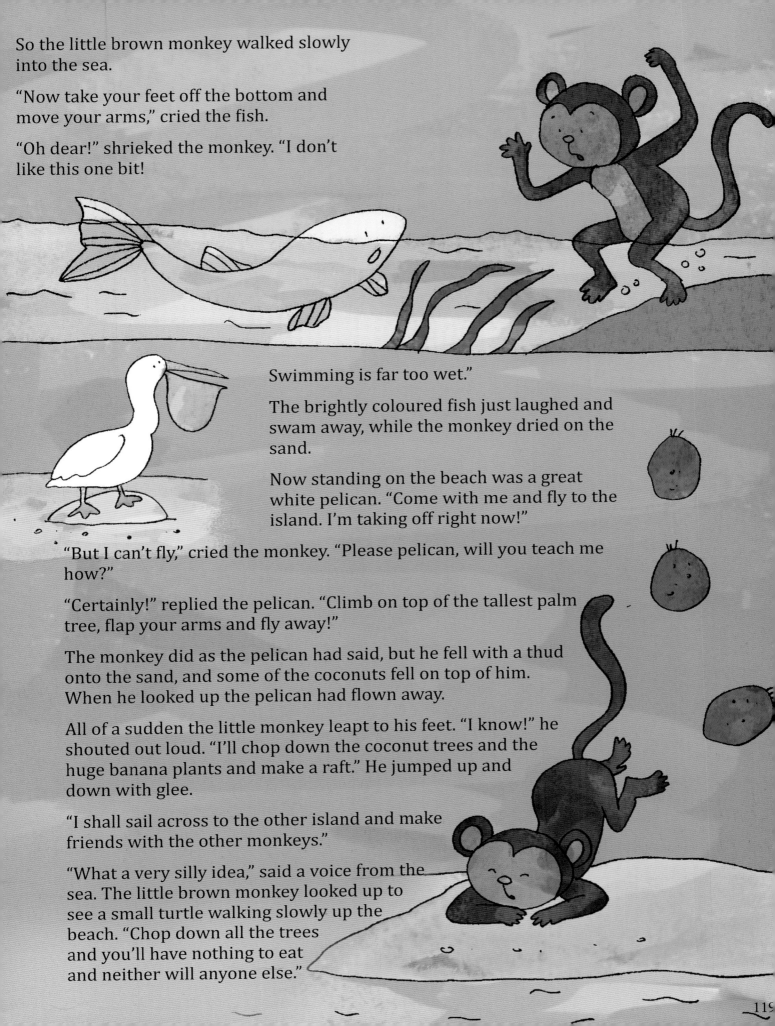

Swimming is far too wet."

The brightly coloured fish just laughed and swam away, while the monkey dried on the sand.

Now standing on the beach was a great white pelican. "Come with me and fly to the island. I'm taking off right now!"

"But I can't fly," cried the monkey. "Please pelican, will you teach me how?"

"Certainly!" replied the pelican. "Climb on top of the tallest palm tree, flap your arms and fly away!"

The monkey did as the pelican had said, but he fell with a thud onto the sand, and some of the coconuts fell on top of him. When he looked up the pelican had flown away.

All of a sudden the little monkey leapt to his feet. "I know!" he shouted out loud. "I'll chop down the coconut trees and the huge banana plants and make a raft." He jumped up and down with glee.

"I shall sail across to the other island and make friends with the other monkeys."

"What a very silly idea," said a voice from the sea. The little brown monkey looked up to see a small turtle walking slowly up the beach. "Chop down all the trees and you'll have nothing to eat and neither will anyone else."

The monkey hung his head. "I don't have an axe!" he muttered.

"Just as well!" the turtle said, shaking his head. "I could take you across to the island on my back, but you're far too big." And with that the small green turtle walked slowly back into the sea.

This made the little brown monkey feel so sad and lonely, that he sat on the sand and cried.

Then all of a sudden, out of the sea, rose the biggest turtle you have ever seen. Very slowly he plodded towards the sad little brown monkey.

"Dry those tears, climb onto my back and don't forget to hold on tight," said the big turtle with a smile.

"You'll never be lonely again when we reach the other island."

The turtle's shell looked so large, the little monkey knew he would be quite safe.

When the little brown monkey looked down into the clear blue sea, what do you think he saw? Bobbing up and down in the water next to them was the little green turtle.

"I knew I was far too small to carry you to the island, so I asked my great-great grandfather to help you. He's very kind and very wise."

"So are you," said the monkey with a smile. "Thank you for everything, little green turtle. I shall never be lonely again."

A Shelf full Of Dolls

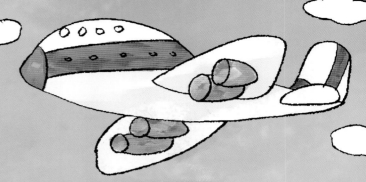

Sarah's daddy had a job at the airport. Most of the time he went to work in the morning and came home every night. But sometimes he flew away to different countries and stayed there for a few days.

Every time he came back from a trip abroad, Sarah's daddy brought her a doll. She had a different doll from every country he visited!

Sarah's daddy had put up some shelves on Sarah's bedroom wall so that she could look at her collection of dolls all the time. One day he added a new shelf next to the others.

·"All ready for the new doll I'll be bringing back from my next trip!" he said.

"It's a very long shelf for one doll!" said Sarah, looking puzzled as she waved her daddy goodbye.

After a week, Daddy returned and brought Sarah the new doll he had promised. And what a strange doll it was. It had no arms or legs, it was made of painted wood and rattled!

"This is a Russian doll," Daddy smiled, as he unscrewed its body and found another doll inside.

Then Sarah unscrewed the second doll and found another. On and on she went until there were nine beautiful Russian dolls, each one a little bit smaller than the other.

"Now I know why you put up such a long shelf!" laughed Sarah, as she placed the dolls in a row.

The Professor's Pencil

Jack lived next door to Professor Smart, who spent all day and most of the night inventing things!

"I wish you could invent something to help me," said Jack with a grin, as he sat outside on the step practising his handwriting in an exercise book.

"I most certainly can!" replied the Professor, and he rushed off to start work straight away.

All that day and most of the next, Jack could hear rattling and banging coming from next door.

"Finished at last!" cried the Professor from over the fence. Jack jumped up at once and ran round to his house to take a look. There in the garden was the strangest machine Jack had ever seen. "What is that?" asked Jack in amazement.

"A machine for making full stops!" said the Professor with pride.

Jack laughed until he cried. "But I can do that easily with one small pencil."

"Oh dear!" sighed the Professor. "Of course you can, what a silly man I am!"

"Never mind," said Jack smiling, "your machine will be perfect for planting Dad's seeds!"

Ossie's Umbrella

Every morning Ossie the ostrich went for a run across the plain. Now, as you know, ostriches can run very fast indeed, but they cannot fly.

Ossie really wanted to fly. "If I run fast enough, one day I may take off and fly up into the air," he thought. Sad to say, he never did!

One fine morning, after a long hard run, Ossie the ostrich stopped for a rest. As he looked down on the ground he spotted a brightly coloured snake.

"Lovely morning for a run!" giggled Ossie, because he knew that snakes never ran anywhere.

When the snake didn't reply, Ossie felt a bit ashamed. "I was only teasing," he said as he bent down to the snake. "Sorry."

Suddenly Ossie heard loud laughter, it was a little rhino who had stopped to see what was happening.

"It's not a snake, you silly ostrich, it's an umbrella!"

As Ossie opened the umbrella and held it high above his head, a strong breeze blew over the plain and gently lifted the startled ostrich into the air.

"I'm flying," gasped Ossie. 'I'm really flying!"

123

The animals below got such a shock as they looked up and saw an ostrich gliding above the tree tops.

A startled crane flew beside Ossie for a while. "Never thought I'd see an ostrich fly," he called. "I'm off to tell my friends about this."

Ossie the ostrich flew around happily all day and when the wind dropped, he floated gently to the ground.

"That was really exciting!" gasped Ossie as he carefully folded up the umbrella. "I shall carry this wherever I go, and when the wind blows I shall be off on another flying adventure!"

The Big Wooden Toy Box

Tom and Rosie-Anne had a great big toy box. It was made of wood, with a lid that made a very loud bang when you closed it!

The toy box was so large that every single one of Tom and Rosie-Anne's toys fitted inside. This is why the children's room was always so tidy and neat.

Their mother loved the wooden toy box, but the toys did not!

"I don't like being in here one little bit!" said the rag doll to one of the soft toys. "The skipping rope gets tangled round my legs, and I have bricks and jigsaw pieces sticking into my back."

"That sounds very painful," whispered one of the teddies, "but what I hate most of all is the dark, when the lid is closed it's very spooky in here!"

"Perhaps if we all pushed hard we could manage to open the lid," suggested the clown. But the lid was far too heavy, so the toys had to stay in the dark.

One Saturday Tom and Rosie-Anne asked their mother if she had a job for them to do.

"Not at the moment," she said, "but Dad may find you one in the garage."

Dad was delighted and found them a job straight away. "Can you tidy up my tools and put them away in those boxes?"

"What a mess!" cried the children as they looked around the garage Tools were scattered all over the floor and piled up under benches.

"I wish I had your big wooden toy box!" said their dad with a sigh.

"All my tools would fit inside, and when I close the lid, everything would look tidy."

This gave Tom and Rosie-Anne an idea. "Will you swap all your small tool boxes for our big wooden one?" the children asked.

"I certainly will!" he agreed at once. "We'll do it straight away."

When the job was finished, everyone was happy. Dad had the big wooden toy box with the lid and his garage was never untidy again.

Tom and Rosie-Anne could still keep their room as tidy as ever, and they could see their toys all the time.

As for the toys, they had much more room, they could look around and they were never shut in the dark again.

Fluffy The Tortoise

Grandad had always told Lottie that when the top of her fluffy hat reached the top of the gate she could have a pet!

"Yippee!" cried Lottie, "I know exactly what I want."

"Come with me to my hen house," said Grandad. "I have a hen with six fluffy chicks. Would you like one of those?"

"They're lovely!" said Lottie, "but I know exactly what I want."

"At the bottom of the garden is a duck with five yellow ducklings. How about one of those?"

"They're great!" said Lottie, "but I know exactly what I want!"

Along came the postwoman with the letters. "I have a cat with three soft kittens. You can choose one of those."

"That's terrific!" said Lottie, "but I know exactly what I want."

Next came the baker bringing the bread. "My dog has four little puppies at home. You can pick one of those if you like."

"How marvellous!" said Lottie, "but I know exactly what I want."

The farmer across the field owned a pony with foals. "Come and take a look, you might like one of those."

"They are beautiful!" said Lottie, "but I know exactly what I want."

In a sty on the farm was a pig with ten little piglets.

"Goodness!" said Lottie. "I couldn't manage even one of those, I know exactly what I want."

Then she went to the pet shop. The man inside said, "Have a good look round before you choose."

"Wonderful!" cried Lottie, "I have found exactly what I want. I want a tortoise!"

Just then a parrot pulled off Lottie's fluffy hat. It dropped right on top of the tortoise.

"Perfect!" cried Lottie, "I shall call you Fluffy the Tortoise. And you are exactly what I want."

Hilda The Hippo

Hilda the hippo lived on the bank of a wide muddy river. All the other hippos liked the edge of the river best, where the mud was thick and sticky like warm melted chocolate.

They even dozed off to sleep in it on hot afternoons, with the top of their heads just showing above the mud.

"Come on in!" cried the rest of Hilda's family. "The mud is lovely!"

But Hilda was not keen on the idea at all, she liked standing in the clean, refreshing rain, especially during a thunderstorm. Best of all she loved to watch the frogs leaping onto the lily pads and floating on top of the water.

"I wish I could do that," Hilda sighed. "Then I would never get muddy!" But each time Hilda tried to fit all four feet onto a lily-pad, she sank like a stone!

Now frogs can be very helpful creatures

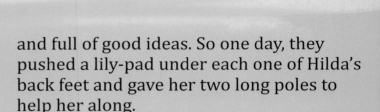

and full of good ideas. So one day, they pushed a lily-pad under each one of Hilda's back feet and gave her two long poles to help her along.

With a bit of practise, Hilda was soon skiing across the water on her lily-pad skis.

It so happened that one day a photographer took Hilda's picture and sent it to a wildlife magazine. Very soon, everyone wanted to see Hilda, the skiing hippo.

"In my country," the photographer told Hilda, "everyone skis all the time! Why don't you come and see for yourself?"

So Hilda left her muddy river and flew far away on an aeroplane. It was very exciting!

When she landed, the little hippo couldn't believe her eyes.

Everywhere was white! Mountains, hills, even streets were covered in thick, fluffy, white snow.

In no time at all, Hilda jumped on a pair of skis and whizzed off down the mountain side. In and out of the trees she sped until she came to an enormous ski jump. Hilda took off, flew through the air, then made a perfect landing at the bottom.

"What a winner!" yelled the crowd. "It's the longest jump ever made!" They gave Hilda a shiny, gold medal.

Hilda stayed a while to ski in the snowy land, and when she returned on the aeroplane, she wore her gold medal around her neck - just to show the frogs on the muddy river back home!

131

The Mole's Adventure

"What a lovely morning," purred Oscar the cat as he stepped outside the front door. "I think I shall take a stroll round the garden."

So Oscar walked down the path, past the flower bed, then walked back again along the top of the fence.

"That's enough exercise for one morning," said Oscar out loud, and jumped down onto the grass.

All of a sudden, a small mound of earth appeared right next to him. "Goodness me," gasped Oscar, "where did that come from?"

From the middle of the earth popped a velvety brown mole.

"Good morning to you!" the mole said with a grin. "I've just come up from my underground burrow in search of an adventure!"

Oscar jumped back up onto the fence in surprise. "What sort of adventure would you like?" he asked the mole.

"I want to climb up on the fence just like you," laughed the mole. "Better still, I would like to climb a tree!"

"Moles can't climb trees," said Oscar with a shake of his head, "but that would be some adventure for you. Just let me think for a minute!"

So Oscar sat on the fence, closed his eyes and thought and thought.

At last he came up with a wonderful idea which he whispered to the mole.

Behind the fence were two apple trees and on the lowest branch of one was a swing. Oscar helped the mole up onto the seat and pushed it until he was swinging higher and higher. Then, quick as a wink, Oscar ran up the other tree and grabbed the mole as he swung near to him.

The two then sat side by side on one of the branches. "Now you have climbed a tree!" laughed Oscar.

"What a great adventure!" gasped the mole, quite out of breath.

Soon a small crowd gathered under the apple tree. "Look!" they shouted pointing up at the branch, "a mole that can climb trees!"

How the two new friends laughed. "Perhaps someone will take our picture," said Oscar, "then you will be able to show everyone how you once really did climb a tree!"

Let's Go On A Picnic

One fine, warm summer's day a few of the woodland folk discussed going on a day out.

"It's a perfect day for a picnic," said the fox, as he gazed up at the clear blue sky.

"Why don't we pack a picnic basket and go on a hike?" suggested two chipmunks, who were always very helpful.

Everyone agreed it was a splendid idea, and ran back home to fetch some food.

In next to no time, the animals were back and the picnic basket full to the brim.

"This basket is rather heavy," said a rabbit, as he tried to lift one corner.

"We can take turns carrying it," suggested one of the helpful chipmunks, "we'll take the first turn!"

So the friends set off. They walked through the wood, down a lane, then across a meadow until they came to a stream.

"Look at that lovely place over there, it's just perfect for a picnic," called the porcupine, as he pointed to a field across the water.

"But how are we going to get across?" cried the animals all together.

"Look, a log has fallen across the stream!" cried the two chipmunks, helpful as ever.

"I'll go first," said the fox. "I have a perfect sense of balance."

"Me next," said the porcupine, who couldn't keep his balance at all.

"If I slip, I shall fall onto the rabbits!"

"Oh no you won't!" cried the rabbits hopping in front. One by one they crossed the log with great care.

How funny the five looked as they wobbled their way along the log trying to keep balance.

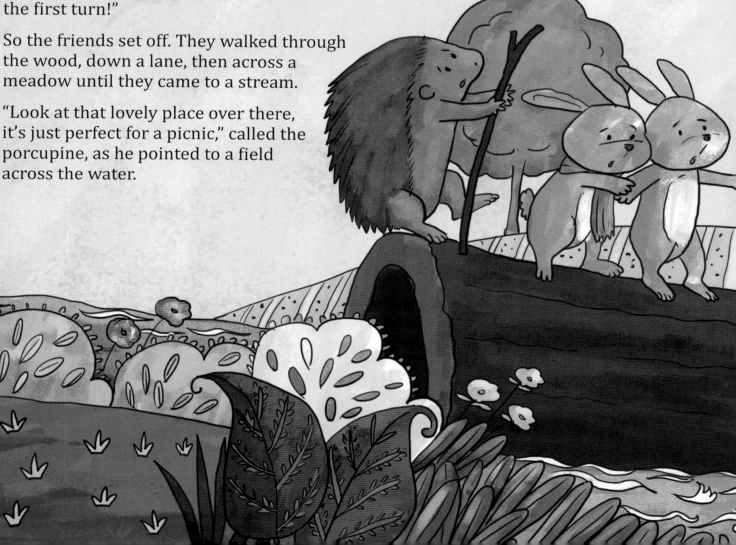

Now while all this was going on, the two helpful little chipmunks had been very busy. Believe it or not, the animals' picnic was already set out in the opposite field.

The chipmunks had noticed that the fallen log was hollow. It was quite big enough for them to scamper through and carry, all the picnic food to the other side. The rabbits, the porcupine and the fox could have gone through the log quite easily, instead of wobbling their way across!

At last the five friends reached the other side of the stream and flopped down on the grass with relief. And what do you think they found? The two chipmunks sitting by the side of the picnic, helpless with laughter!

Later on when the picnic was over, everybody went back through the hollow log with no trouble at all!

The two little chipmunks led the way, and helpful as ever, carried the empty picnic basket back home.

Matilda Is Missing

Matilda went everywhere with Maggie. Matilda was Maggie's favourite doll and when Maggie went out, she took Matilda with her zipped up safely in her own special bag.

One day Maggie went for a walk across the park with Matilda's zip-bag slung over her shoulder.

"How about a swing?" Maggie asked as she unzipped Matilda's special bag.

Poor Maggie gasped! The bag was empty! She yelled at the top of her voice. "Matilda is missing!"

She shouted so loudly that everyone in the park could hear. In fact, Maggie's voice was so noisy, that everyone in the town could hear her too.

Even Maggie's mother could hear her cry, "Matilda is missing!" although she was inside the house. As fast as possible, Maggie's mother ran upstairs and saw there Matilda the doll sitting on Maggie's bed. She had slipped from the bag and was safe at home all the time.

"What a silly girl I am!" said Maggie when she found out, and her face went very red indeed!

The Lonely Little Lighthouse

In the middle of the sea, perched safely on top of the rocks, stood a little lighthouse. His light shone far out to sea, but no ship had passed by for years. So one day, the lighthouse keeper said goodbye and left him all alone.

This made the little lighthouse feel very sad. "I'm no use to anyone anymore," he sobbed. "My light will soon go out and I'll be forgotten!"

Now some of the seals and walruses who visited the rocks heard the lonely lighthouse. So they put their heads together, and very soon thought of a way to cheer him up.

"We can take it in turns to be the lighthouse keeper and work the light!" suggested the biggest walrus.

The little lighthouse liked the sound of this and began to brighten up right away.

So every night, when darkness falls over the sea, the little lighthouse shines his light. Then the dolphins, the seals and the walruses, sometimes even a couple of whales, come out to play.

Everyone has a wonderful time, especially the little lighthouse. His light shines in the dark like a star and he is never ever lonely.

Jolly Monster's Birthday

It was Jolly Monster's birthday and he was giving a great big birthday party. All his monster friends had been invited and Jolly Monster was hoping for some very large presents, but what he wanted most of all was a big surprise.

That afternoon when the Jolly Monster's friends arrived for tea, each one was carrying a great big box. Jolly Monster could hardly wait to open them.

In the first box was an enormous pair of trainers with red laces.

"I could run a marathon in these!" chuckled Jolly Monster.

When he opened the next box, he found a tee-shirt, not quite the right size!

Most of his friends had brought useful things, like a huge pairs of socks, gigantic gloves, but he received a hat that was far too small!

Some brought games and large balloons that could be seen from far away.

There were sacks full of sweets and lollipops as tall as trees.

All of a sudden someone yelled, "Hide your eyes Jolly Monster, here comes the big surprise!"

Speeding across the lawn came a lorry loaded down with... What do you think?

The biggest blow up castle you have ever seen. Just perfect for Jolly Monster and his friends to bounce up and down on all day!

"I wished for a big surprise, and this is just perfect!" laughed Jolly Monster, as he jumped up into the air.

Bobby Gets Dressed

Little Bobby Briggs was a very good boy, except for one thing. He would not get dressed in the morning!

When the alarm clock rang at eight o'clock, Bobby would jump out of bed straight away, run to the bathroom, wash, clean his teeth and comb his hair but - he would not get dressed in the morning!

This made everyone very cross as well as very late.

One day his sister Susie thought of a good idea. She put all Bobby's clothes for that day into a pillow case and then played his favourite tune on his toy xylophone.

"When the music stops," Susie told her little brother, "take something out of the pillow case and put it on!"

Bobby thought this was a great game and couldn't wait to join in.

First he took out his hat, and when the music stopped again he put on a sock. Next came his vest, then another sock, then pants and a shirt, and very soon he was dressed to go out.

What a good idea sister Susie! Are you going to play this game with Bobby every time he goes out?

141

Racing Rabbit

A postcard came one day for Wise Rabbit. It was from his long lost cousins who lived half way across the world.

'Do come and visit us as soon as you can,' the message read. Wise Rabbit thought this a good idea.

"It's rather a long way," Wise Rabbit said, "but if I can find someone to mow my lawn and look after my garden shed, I shall go at once!"

The neighbours said, "Ask any one of us to mow your lawn and look after your garden shed, but whatever you do, don't ask Bunny Hopkins!"

This made Wise Rabbit think long and hard.

The very next day when Bunny Hopkins passed by, Wise Rabbit gave him the key to the garden shed.

"Leave everything to me!" said Bunny Hopkins eagerly. "I will mow your lawn every week and guard your garden shed with my life."

Off went Wise Rabbit to visit his cousins, but sadly, Bunny Hopkins did not keep his promise.

All summer long he sat in the garden sunbathing. The grass on the lawn grew tall and the weeds almost covered the garden shed.

"I think it's about time I mowed the lawn!" said Bunny Hopkins with a yawn.

When at last the young rabbit unlocked the garden shed, he was in for a big surprise! For standing next to the mower was the biggest motorbike he had ever seen.

On top of the seat was a note which read, 'When you have finished mowing the lawn, use my bike as often as you like.'

Poor Bunny Hopkins just stood and stared. "If I'd mowed the lawn each week as I'd promised, I could have ridden the bike all summer!" he cried.

How quickly Bunny Hopkins got to work, and at last when all the jobs were finished, he raced off on Wise Rabbit's magnificent motorbike.

"Soon Wise Rabbit will be back," sighed Bunny Hopkins, "and I won't be able to ride the motorbike ever again!"

But on the very day he was due to return, Bunny Hopkins received a postcard. It was from Wise Rabbit!

The card was addressed to 'Bunny Hopkins, The Racing Rabbit', and this is what it said: 'I am going to stay here until next year. Please mow my lawn, look after my garden shed and don't forget to ride my motorbike!' Bunny Hopkins was delighted.

Terry's first Prize

Terry drove a yellow taxi all day long. The city streets were very busy with lots of noisy traffic, which often gave Terry a headache.

"Sometimes I wish I lived in a place with no cars at all," he sighed.

One day a man knocked on Terry's door. "You have won first in our great competition!"

Terry looked pleased. "Is it a desert island?" he asked the man.

"I'll give you a clue!" the man smiled. "It has four wheels and travels on the road."

Terry's face fell. "I hope it's not a car!" he cried. He soon cheered up when he saw his very own gipsy caravan!

Mrs Bruno's Pies

Mrs Bruno baked marvellous hot cherry pies. They tasted so good that everyone wanted to buy them. Before long Mrs Bruno's hot cherry pies became famous.

"What am I going to do?" asked Mrs Bruno, looking worried.

"I love to bake cherry pies, but when I stop to answer the door, the pies in the oven get burnt, and I have so far to walk to my customers, that my pies are cold by the time they are delivered."

What a problem!

"I think I shall have to stop baking my hot cherry pies!"

"What! No more pies?" cried the customers. So they got together and came up with a splendid idea. They would come and collect the pies from Mrs Bruno's house.

Now Mrs Bruno can bake her famous hot cherry pies, and everyone is happy!

The Musical Mouse

Morgan the mouse made no noise at all. "You really are as quiet as a mouse Morgan!" everyone said with a smile.

"Mice are naturally quiet creatures," nodded Morgan wisely.

Then he scampered off without so much as a rustle or a squeak.

Now one day, as Morgan was sitting perfectly still by the side of the road, he heard a wonderful sound. As he listened the sound grew louder and louder.

"It's coming nearer!" shouted Morgan at the top of his voice, which was very unlike him.

Just then the town band came round the corner playing catchy tunes on their instruments.

Morgan had never heard music before and knew he had to join in.

"I've been so quiet all my life," yelled Morgan as he ran alongside the players, "I want to make a great big noise!"

"Try these cymbals," said the cat. Morgan crashed them together so hard that the band almost fell over one another.

"Try this trombone," suggested the dog. Morgan played so hard he almost blew the band away.

Next he tried the drums and made such a noise that the elephants ran behind a wall in fright.

"I thought mice were supposed to be quiet creatures!" whispered one of the band.

"We are!" Morgan agreed as he banged hard on a tambourine, "but making a noise is such wonderful fun!"

By now the band was in a muddle. They were playing different tunes and everyone was bumping into each other.

Suddenly the band leader shouted above the din. "You can be leader of the band Morgan, then everybody can get back to making music instead of a noise!"

Honey Bear's Promise

Honey Bear was very fond of sweet things to eat. He loved jam and candy bars, sticky gingerbread and sugary biscuits - but most of all he loved honey! Every morning, he spread it thickly on hot toast. At lunch time he let it trickle all over his pancakes, and at tea he gobbled up a huge plateful of tasty honey sandwiches.

Now Mother Bear kept the honey on the very top shelf of the kitchen cupboard. The shelf was far too high for Honey Bear to reach unless he climbed to the top of Father's wooden steps.

One day, when he thought no one was looking, Honey Bear carried Father's wooden steps into the kitchen.

"If I'm very quiet and ever so careful, I can climb up and reach the honey jar from the top shelf," Honey Bear chuckled to himself. But when Honey Bear got almost to the top, the steps began to wobble and shake which gave the little bear quite a fright.

"Help! Help!" yelled Honey Bear as he clung onto the steps.

Luckily, Father Bear was behind the kitchen door and caught Honey Bear before he fell off and hurt himself.

Father Bear looked very cross. "You must promise never to climb the steps," he said sternly, "it's far too dangerous!"

Honey Bear hung his head and promised.

The very next day when Honey Bear looked longingly at that big jar of honey, he remembered his promise.

Then all of a sudden he had a wonderful idea. "I know how to reach the honey, without using Father's steps at all!"

So very carefully he opened the bottom drawer of the cupboard, then the next drawer, and the next, and so on, until he could reach that tempting jar of honey.

Honey Bear slowly climbed down with the precious jar tucked safely in his paw. He reached for a spoon from the top drawer of the cupboard, then settled down to enjoy the lovely honey!

The Runaround Clock

The alarm clock on the bedroom shelf opened his eyes and looked around. Dawn was breaking and the first rays of the sun were just peeping through the curtains.

"I'm bored!" the clock ticked.

"Everyone is still fast asleep. I've been ticking away all through the night, and no-one has listened to a single tic toc!"

"That's what clocks are supposed to do!" snapped a china dog on the shelf, "just tic-toe away all night and all day."

"Well, it's very boring!" replied the alarm clock crossly. "No-one listens to me· until eight o'clock when my alarm bell rings!"

The alarm clock looked down at his hands. "It's only five o'clock. I think I shall go for a run." And with that he jumped off the shelf and ran downstairs.

Once outside, the alarm clock dashed off quickly down the street. He hadn't gone very far when a small dog, out for his early morning walk, barked and growled at the poor alarm clock. The dog chased him across the road, where a boy delivering newspapers almost ran over him with his bicycle wheel.

Then, without any warning, a machine that cleans the street, sprayed him with cold water and whisked him along the gutter with its whirring brushes.

"Oh dear me!" gasped the alarm clock, looking down at his hands. "It's six o'clock. I've only been outside an hour. How I wish I was back on the shelf at home."

But there was worse to come! The man who drove the dustcart saw the alarm clock upside down in the gutter. He thought it was a piece of junk and threw him onto his cart!

"Look at the time!" gasped the alarm clock as he looked at his hands. "It's almost five minutes to eight!"

With one last effort he ran upstairs, jumped back on bedroom shelf and rang his bell as hard as he could.

'Time to get up!" cried one of the family. "It's exactly eight o'clock and our alarm clock is right on time as usual!"

The dustcart travelled round the streets for ages collecting more and more rubbish. At last the alarm clock struggled to the top of the pile and peered out of the back of the cart.

To his great delight he was only two doors away from his own house, so he jumped down from the cart and rolled into his very own garden.

The cat, who had been out all night, sniffed at the alarm clock, then pushed him over with her paw.

Who Has Eaten The Garden?

In spring (when the weather begins to turn warm), Lucy and Grandma spent hours planting vegetable seeds in the garden.

Lucy thought they took ages to grow, but one morning in summer Grandma said that at last they were ready for picking.

"Let's have peas today!" said Lucy. "They're my favourite!"

So she took a bowl into the garden and filled it with fresh green pea-pods. Then she sat outside the kitchen door and shelled the peas for lunch - perhaps she ate one or two as well!

The next day Lucy chose carrots for lunch, but when she went out to pick them, she found that something had been nibbling the garden. Most of the vegetables had been eaten! Whatever could it be?

"It must be rabbits!" said the milkman. 'They love carrots."

"It can't be," said Lucy. "I give them plenty of lettuce and cabbage leaves!"

"It must be pigeons!" said the postman. "They love peas."

"Never!" cried Lucy. "I give them corn and crumbs all the time."

"Then, it's slugs!" said the boy returning from school. "They'll eat anything."

"Oh dear!" sighed Lucy. "What shall we do?"

"Make a scarecrow," suggested Grandad. "We'll do it this afternoon."

Next morning, as soon as it was light, Lucy crept downstairs and tiptoed into the vegetable garden. What a surprise she got! Not rabbits, not pigeons, not even slugs - but a baby deer nibbling beans and making friends with the scarecrow.

Very quietly, Lucy crept up to the deer and stroked his nose.

"So it was you who ate the garden," she whispered. "I wish I could keep you as a pet."

Grandad shook his head. I'm sure if you put out some food, the little deer will come out of the wood to see you sometimes," he said with a smile. "As long as he leaves our vegetables alone!"

The Animal Olympics

Once a year the animals held a meeting. They talked about this and that, told one another all their news, then everyone joined in a gigantic party.

Now this year they wanted to do something quite different, so they decided to hold the Animal Olympics!

"We'll all meet back here one week from now," suggested the elephant. "Then everyone can take part and try to win a gold medal."

"How exciting!" cried all the animals, and they ran off at once to practise.

How hard the animals tried. They practised the long jump and the high jump, the javelin and the pole vault. The monkeys tried to throw the discus· and shot put - but they didn't get very far.

"I'm the fastest animal in the world," sobbed Cheetah. "If I take part I shall win all the races, and it will be no fun at all!"

"Cheer up!" said the Hippo. "I have the perfect job for a fast runner like you. Will you carry the Olympic torch and start the games?"

The cheetah was delighted and stopped crying at once.

The day of the Animal Olympic Games came at last. The animals arrived looking very smart in their sports clothes, all except one. Tommy Tortoise stood on his own looking very sad. "I've practised everyday, but I'm far too slow to take part in any event;" he sobbed.

"Not to worry!" said the Hippo. "We need someone to fire the starting pistol and time the races."

Tommy Tortoise cheered up at once and plodded off to the starting point.

All of a sudden, one of the other animals began sniffing. It was the cheetah.

"Why are you crying too?" asked the Hippo rather surprised.

At last the Animal Olympics began. They lasted all day long, and each animal won a medal for one event or another.

Everyone went home late that evening feeling very happy and very tired - especially the tortoise and the cheetah!

The Rocky Mountain Train

Once upon a time there was a Red Train which carried people across the Rocky Mountains.

Everyday the Red Train had to pull lots of carriages, because so many people wanted to cross the mountains to the other side. Slowly, the Red Train huffed and puffed his way over the mountains with his load getting heavier and heavier everyday.

"My goodness!" said the engine driver, when he saw more and more people waiting at the station each morning. "If I add any more carriages, the Red Train will break down one day!"

Now the Red Train kept going because he liked to make the passengers happy, and he loved to listen to the song they sang on the journey across the Rocky Mountains.

"Through the mountain we will go,

In the rain and frost and snow.

The bright Red Train will be our guide,

Until we reach the other side.

Merrily he'll puff along,

Until we end this happy song!"

One morning, there were even more people than usual waiting at the station. Very soon the Red Train's carriages were packed full of passengers.

The Red Train pulled very slowly out of the station, but as soon as he started to cross the mountains, he huffed and puffed, blew his whistle and came to a stop.

"Poor Red Train," said his engine driver. "He's too tired to go any further!"

"Oh dear!" cried all the passengers. "This is our fault. What can we do?"

All of a sudden a little boy jumped down from the train and shouted to the passengers leaning out of the carriage windows.

"The song we always sing says 'through the mountains we will go', perhaps the Red Train used to go through the mountains and there is a hidden tunnel somewhere - that would save going up and over them!"

The Red Train blew his whistle very hard, he could just remember going through the tunnel many years ago.

At once the passengers climbed out of the train, they searched round the mountain until at last they found the opening of the old tunnel.

Everyone worked very hard pulling away tangled undergrowth and clearing the track.

Very soon the Red Train was speeding happily through the tunnel, straight through the mountains in next to no time. The passengers sang the Red Train's very own song at the tops of their voices!

Jed's Special Sweater

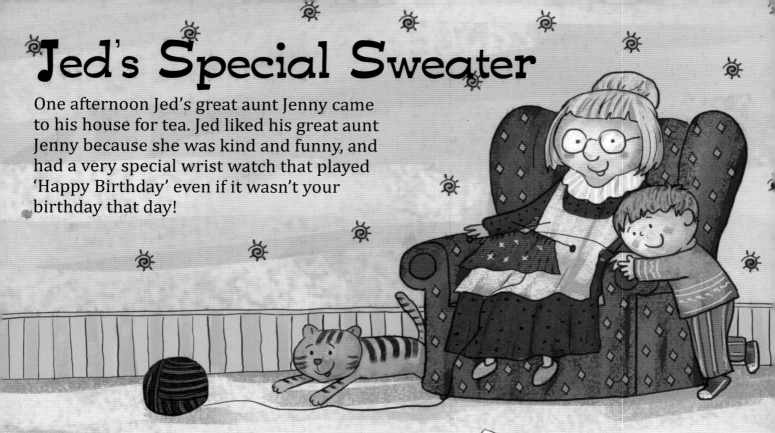

One afternoon Jed's great aunt Jenny came to his house for tea. Jed liked his great aunt Jenny because she was kind and funny, and had a very special wrist watch that played 'Happy Birthday' even if it wasn't your birthday that day!

After tea, Great Aunt Jenny asked Jed if she could borrow a book about space travel. Jed had lots, so he gave her a book full of pictures of spacemen, rockets and the moon.

Next time Great Aunt Jenny came to tea she was carrying a brown paper parcel.

"For you Jed!" she said with a smile. "I hope you like it!"

Inside the parcel Jed found a lovely bright red sweater. On the front Great Aunt Jenny had carefully knitted a picture of a spaceman in his helmet, with a silver rocket in the background.

"Just like the picture in your book," laughed Great Aunt Jenny as Jed pulled on his wonderful sweater.

He was delighted with his present and wanted to wear it every day. He tried very hard not to get it dirty, because he missed his sweater so much when it had to be washed.

Every Thursday Jed and his school friends went to the swimming pool with their teacher. After the swimming lesson, all the children rushed into the changing rooms to get dried and dressed.

"Quick as you can, children!" called their teacher. "The bus is waiting to take you back to school."

Quickly Jed pulled on his clothes, tied his shoes, then hunted round for his special sweater. At last he spotted it under a bench on the wet floor. Fast as he could, Jed tugged on his sweater, then hurried onto the bus with all the others.

Later that afternoon, as Jed was walking home, he looked down at his sweater and got quite a shock. The front was plain red and the spacemen with his rocket had vanished.

"Oh no!" gasped poor Jed, almost in tears. "I must have put on the wrong sweater!"

When he got home Great Aunt Jenny was there. "I've lost my spaceman sweater," sobbed Jed.

All of a sudden Great Aunt Jenny began to smile and Jed's mother laughed out loud.

"Your sweater's back to front," giggled Great Aunt Jenny. "Come here, you silly boy," and she turned Jed's sweater around, so the spaceman and the rocket were at the front for everyone to see!

Teddy's Soup

Teddy Bear had a problem, he was very bad at spelling.

"I do try really hard!" he told Mother Bear. "In fact, I am busy reading my book right now."

Mother Bear smiled to herself when she noticed that Teddy was holding his book upside down.

Then she thought of a bright idea. Mother Bear went into the kitchen straight away and made Teddy a large bowl of alphabet soup.

"Now you can learn your letters as you eat," she laughed.

The alphabet tasted so good, that Teddy emptied the bowl in one gulp.

"Perhaps that wasn't such a good idea after all," chuckled Mother Bear, as she filled Teddy's bowl up with soup once more!

Cathy's Tea Party

One afternoon, deep down at the bottom of the ocean, Cathy the crab was giving a tea party.

That morning she had made lots of iced buns, a very fancy cake and two huge plates of seaweed sandwiches.

In the afternoon when she laid the table, Cathy set out eight plates and eight cups and saucers.

"How many guests are coming to the tea party?" asked a cheeky little fish passing by.

"I've invited one guest," giggled Cathy. "It's Ollie the Octopus!"

"I need a plate for each of my eight arms," laughed Ollie as he put a delicious cake onto each plate.

Mike The Mixer

Mike the mixer was brand new. His orange paintwork gleamed, his mixer was spotless, even his tyres were perfectly clean.

It was Mike the mixer's first day out and he was longing to get dirty. "I hope lots of people will want cement," he said to himself, as he drove along the road to find some work.

He hadn't travelled very far before he came to some major roadworks. On the left was a long queue of trucks and lorries waiting to dump their loads.

"Have you brought any stone or tarmac to put on the roads?" shouted the man in charge.

"Nothing at all," replied Mike, "but I'll fetch you a load of cement."

"Don't bother," said the man. "We don't need any here. Now get out of the way!"

So Mike. the mixer hurried on until he came to a building site.
"This looks promising," he said to himself, as he parked beside
a pile of bricks and some sand.

"Can I fetch you a load of cement?" Mike called to a bricklayer
building a wall.

"Too late," yelled the man. "We've almost finished for today.
Can you move, you're blocking the way?"

Quickly Mike drove on and turned down the next road where he
found a man laying a new path in his garden.

When he saw Mike, the man shouted across, "I've just mixed all this
concrete myself and now I've got blisters and backache. You should
have come an hour ago!"

"Oh dear!" thought Mike as he drove on. "I won't find any work
there."

All the next week Mike tried to find something to do, but nobody
wanted a load of cement.

Mike was feeling very sorry for himself, so he drove around until he found a quiet street. He gave a deep sigh and switched off his engine.

At that very moment, Mike heard a loud voice right beside him. "You're just what I need. A cement mixer is the answer to all my problems!" A very excited baker was standing next to him, for Mike had parked right outside his shop.

"Today I must bake the tallest birthday cake in the world," the busy baker explained. "I don't have a bowl big enough to mix the cake and my poor arms will ache with all that stirring. Will you help me out?"

Mike the cement mixer was thrilled - a job at last!

The busy baker got to work at once. He loaded butter, sugar, flour and dried fruit into Mike's mixer. Then he tossed in one hundred eggs and a whole box of spices.

Mike started his engine and his mixer began to turn. The busy baker shouted, "Whoa!" when he thought everything was ready. Then Mike tilted his mixer and poured the cake-mix into eleven giant cake tins.

The cakes took hours to bake. When they were ready and had cooled, the baker decorated them with pink sugar icing, while Mike watched through the shop door.

"Who ordered such a giant cake?" Mike asked the baker that night.

"I've no idea!" replied the busy baker, shaking his head. "We shall find out tomorrow."

And find out they did! Next morning the zoo keeper arrived with some of his staff to take the giant cake back with them to the zoo.

"Today is our giraffe's birthday and we wanted a cake as tall as him!"

The baker and Mike were invited to the zoo and asked to join the party.

"Could you stay and work for me and mix cakes instead of cement?" the baker asked Mike.

Mike the cake mixer agreed at once!

The Counting Caterpillar

Some caterpillars like to munch leaves and stalks all day, while others nibble fruit and flowers.

Colin the caterpillar was different. He loved to count!

To begin with, he counted from one to ten. It wasn't long before he could count up to a hundred.

As Colin crawled slowly along he counted the world around him; one bud on a rose, two wings on a wasp, three bugs in a jar, four wings on a dragonfly, five grubs in a peach, six legs on a cricket, seven stripes on a beetle, eight legs on a spider, nine leaves on a plant and ten petals on a daisy.

Colin counted all day long. He counted the insects buzzing around him and the ants as they marched through the long grass.

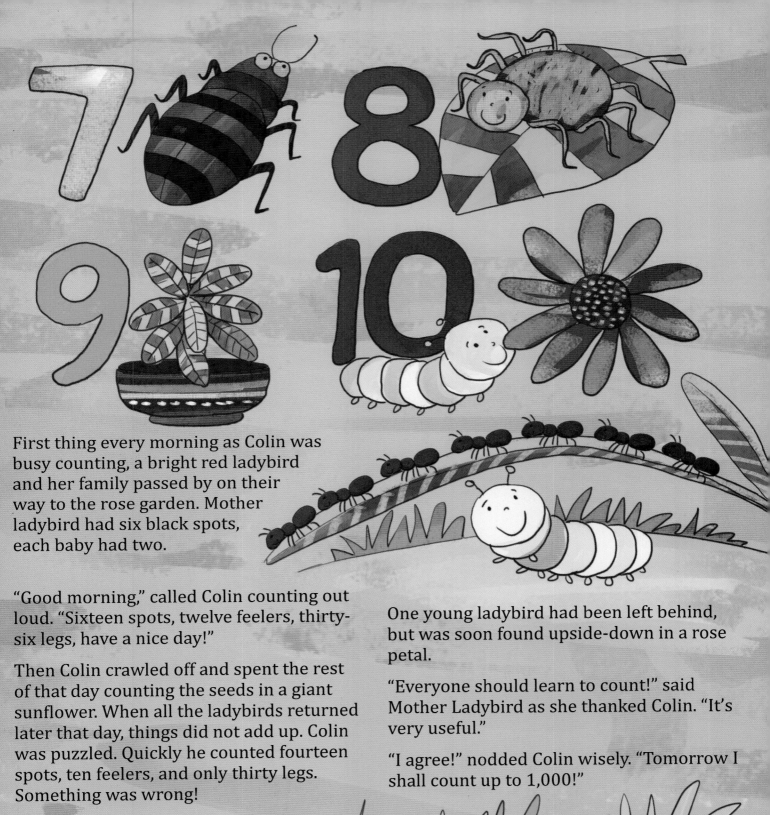

First thing every morning as Colin was busy counting, a bright red ladybird and her family passed by on their way to the rose garden. Mother ladybird had six black spots, each baby had two.

"Good morning," called Colin counting out loud. "Sixteen spots, twelve feelers, thirty-six legs, have a nice day!"

Then Colin crawled off and spent the rest of that day counting the seeds in a giant sunflower. When all the ladybirds returned later that day, things did not add up. Colin was puzzled. Quickly he counted fourteen spots, ten feelers, and only thirty legs. Something was wrong!

One young ladybird had been left behind, but was soon found upside-down in a rose petal.

"Everyone should learn to count!" said Mother Ladybird as she thanked Colin. "It's very useful."

"I agree!" nodded Colin wisely. "Tomorrow I shall count up to 1,000!"

The Pumpkin Man

One day in spring Joe the gardener planted some seeds in his vegetable plot. Joe's cat and dog and even his white rabbit lent a hand.

"When the autumn comes," said Joe, "we shall have plenty of pumpkins!"

Joe was absolutely right. At harvest time his garden was full of ripe orange pumpkins of every shape and size.

Joe, his cat and dog and even his white rabbit had never seen so many pumpkins.

"I shall pick the biggest one," said Joe proudly, "and we shall have pumpkin pie every day."

"Ugh!" groaned Joe's cat and dog and even his rabbit, because they hated the stuff!

So all that day Joe baked pumpkin pies. He cooked so many they filled the kitchen, but still he had only used up half his biggest pumpkin.

"Time to eat," shouted Joe, as he cut for the cat and dog, and even the white rabbit, a huge slice of pumpkin pie.

"But we hate pumpkin pie!" cried the cat,

the dog and even the rabbit.

"And so do I," agreed Joe, when he took his first bite.

"So what can we do with all these pumpkins?" the four friends shouted together.

It was the white rabbit who thought of the best idea.

"Tomorrow is Halloween," he told the others, "everyone will need lots and lots of pumpkins."

So this is what they did.

The rest of that day, Joe and his cat, dog and rabbit, cut and carved the pumpkins ready for Halloween.

When darkness fell, they put a candle in every pumpkin shell and hung them outside the house and all over the garden.

What a beautiful sight hundreds of golden lanterns made with their bright lights flickering in the darkness.

Very soon a huge crowd gathered outside Joe's house. People saw the glowing pumpkin lamps as they passed, and everyone wanted to buy one to take home.

By midnight all the pumpkins had been sold and everyone was happy.

"I love Halloween," sighed the white rabbit, "but best of all I love the pumpkin lanterns."

"Oh my goodness," gasped Joe to his cat and dog. "I'm afraid we've sold the last one."

So the next day, on Halloween, they had to go out and buy a pumpkin - just for the white rabbit.

The Little Red Helicopter

Right on the edge! of a busy airport stood the Little Red Helicopter.

All day long he watched the huge jet planes taking off and landing on the runway, as they carried passengers to far away places.

"It must be wonderful taking people on holiday," sighed the Little Red Helicopter, "but nobody ever notices me!"

Every morning the Little Red Helicopter flew businessmen into the city to work and brought them back to the same place every night It was very dull. No-one ever smiled at the Little Red Helicopter or thanked him for a nice flight His passengers ignored him, they were far too busy to notice the Little Red Helicopter.

Now one morning something different happened. A worried looking gentleman came running towards the Little Red Helicopter.

"Can you take off and land in a very small place?" the gentleman shouted loudly. "Will you please come to our rescue?"

The Little Red Helicopter was overjoyed. Adventure at last! He agreed at once.

Straight away, the staff from the airport pulled out the Little Red Helicopter's seats and began to fill up the space with sacks and bales of hay. How they scratched and tickled the poor Little Red Helicopter.

The pilot climbed in and started the engine, the blades began to spin and soon they were flying high over the airport.

"We must travel across country and up into the hills!" shouted the pilot above all the noise. "Do you think you can land with such a heavy load?"

"I think I can," whirred the Little Red Helicopter. "I'll do my very best."

When he reached the hills the Little Red Helicopter looked down.

There were floods everywhere! The countryside below him was covered with water and the animals had been moved to higher ground. At last the Little Red Helicopter reached the hillside and landed carefully on a very small space.

Everyone clapped and cheered and shouted, "Well done!" They crowded round the Little Red Helicopter and made him feel like a hero.

The animals hadn't eaten for two whole days. Soon they were tucking into the food that the Little Red Helicopter had brought such a long way.

"You've saved the day," said the pilot with a smile. "Would you like to be a rescue helicopter from now on?"

The Little Red Helicopter lifted right off the ground with pride. The very next day the pilot painted the words 'Rescue Helicopter' in black on his side.

The Clowns' Breakfast

Three funny circus clowns lived together in one house. One clown washed the clothes, one clown cooked the meals and the other clown kept the house neat and tidy. Most of the time they got on very well, but there was one thing that they could not agree upon.

Every morning before they went to work at the circus, the three funny clowns would have breakfast together.

They all drank fresh coffee with cream and sugar. They all ate hot toast with butter and jam, but most of all they enjoyed boiled eggs in their very own egg cups.

Each morning the three funny clowns sat round the table listening to their eggs as they bubbled in the pan.

After exactly four minutes the eggs were ready - and that was when the trouble began!

"That's my egg, put it down!"

"Mine was white, yours is brown!"

"They're just the same, put my egg back!"

"Don't mix them up, they're sure to crack!"

The three funny clowns could never agree which egg was which.

That was a pity because their eggs got cold, their toast was burnt and their coffee tasted terrible.

Breakfast was spoiled every day!

"This is no way for three clowns to behave," said the three friends as they gazed at each other sadly.

Suddenly one of the clowns jumped up. "All this fuss over three boiled eggs," he cried, as he pulled a pencil from a pocket in his big baggy trousers. "I have the answer to our problem!"

He picked up one of the eggs and drew a clown's face on it, exactly like his own.

Then the other two clowns did the same.

Now, every morning, each clown draws his own face on his egg before popping it into the pan.

When the eggs are ready there are no more problems, just three happy, hungry clowns.

173

Sam The Scribbling Snake

One day as Sam the Snake slithered along the floor of the steamy jungle, he found a big box of sharp, shiny pencils.

"Super," hissed Sam. "What a simply smashing surprise!" With that, he picked up a pencil and began to scribble.

First he scribbled in the sand, then he scribbled on the flowers and leaves. Next he scribbled up and down the tree trunks. He even scribbled all over the animals.

Something had to be done!

"Sam has lots of pencils," said the baby elephant, "we must find him lots of paper to scribble on!"

Before very long, the animals came back with notebooks and pads of every shape and size and sheets and sheets of paper.

"Stupendous!" Sam hissed happily. "I'll start slowly by spelling short sentences. Soon I shall scribble short stories about all my friends in the jungle."

Sam scribbled so many stories that some were made into books and films, and very soon Sam the Scribbling Snake became a Superstar!

The Sound Asleep Pig

Patti the pig could not get up in the morning. The bell on her alarm clock rang loudly at seven o'clock, but Patti didn't hear a thing.

At eight o'clock, the rooster from the farmyard perched on top of her bed and crowed as loud as he could for half an hour. Still Patti the pig did not wake up!

"I'll try too!" said the owl, and he hooted from nine until ten. Then he flew home to sleep for the day.

Will nothing wake Patti the pig?

At eleven o'clock, the old grey, donkey stuck his head through her bedroom window. He brayed loudly in Patti's ear, until everybody begged him to stop.

How can Patti the pig sleep through all that noise - will she never wake up?

At twelve o'clock the farmer's wife said, "I know how to wake her up!"

She opened Patti's door and shouted, "Dinner time!" In a flash Patti was awake and ready for her dinner.

Now we all know how to wake Patti the sound asleep pig!

Dolly's Telephone

One morning as Dolly was looking in her mirror she gave a little scream. Her face was covered in spots!

"Oh dear! Oh dear!" said the doctor, shaking his head. "You must stay in bed for a whole week."

"But I don't feel in the least bit ill," wailed Dolly, and she went to bed and sulked.

The other toys tried to cheer her up. They came round to visit her.

They brought books and games and flowers and chocolates, which they left outside her bedroom door.

"I shall have no-one to talk to for a whole week!" snapped Dolly, and she pulled the bedclothes over her head.

All the toys felt sorry for Dolly, but they didn't want to go near her just in case they caught the spots too.

"I think I know how to help," piped up a tinkling little voice.

It was the toy telephone. "I will go to visit Dolly this afternoon. She can talk to her friends for an hour and that will cheer her up!"

Dolly was thrilled to see the toy telephone and began to dial straight away. "I have friends all over the world," said Dolly proudly. "Now I can phone every one of them!"

"Oh dear," sighed the toy telephone. "It looks as if I shall be here all week!"

Buzz Builds A Snowman

One winter's day, when the snow lay deep in the garden, William asked his friend, Buzz the Robot, if he would like to make a snowman.

"I don't know how! I don't know how!" whirred Buzz.

"Watch me!" laughed William. "It's very easy!"

So William set to work shovelling the soft snow and piling it up high. He shaped the snow very carefully until he had made a perfect snowman.

"All he needs now is a scarf, some gloves and a hat," smiled William as he stepped back to admire his work. "Now you try Buzz!"

The little robot stared at William's snowman, and all his lights flashed on and off. "Not like that! Not like that!" he cried in his funny robot voice.

He whizzed into the house and came back with a bowl of fruit! This made William howl with laughter.

All of a sudden Buzz whirled his robot arms and there was his snowman made in a flash.

"Looks just like me! Looks just like me!" Buzz giggled, as he pointed to his snowman.

"The bowl of fruit was a great idea," said William. "Only a robot could think of that!"

The Flying Field Mice

Tim and Tilly Field Mouse were sitting in a cornfield gazing up at the bright blue sky. As they watched the clouds floating by, Tilly spotted something.

Flying high above them was a helicopter. As it came nearer, Tim spotted something else. Look!" he squeaked, pointing up into the sky, "someone has jumped out!"

Tim and Tilly Field Mouse held their breath, then all of a sudden a parachute opened up and a man floated gently to the ground.

I wish we could ride in a helicopter and go parachuting," said Tilly, with a sigh, but we're far too small!"

When Tilly looked round Tim was gone. He had scampered up to the top of a hill where a tall sycamore tree grew. Underneath the tree, the ground was covered with sycamore seeds - just like tiny wings.

"Look at me Tilly!" cried Tim, as he jumped into the air. Have you ever seen a flying field mouse before?"

What fun both little mice had.

They flew around all afternoon, until they were tired out.

"Let's go flying again tomorrow," laughed Tilly, as the two field mice went home to bed.

The Monster On The Moon

There were once two little squirrels who lived high up in an old oak tree.

On dark nights, the thing they liked to do most, was to watch the moon from their bedroom window.

"Is there really a Man in the Moon?" they asked Father Squirrel time after time.

So one night he brought his big, brass telescope up to the squirrels' bedroom. "See for yourself!" smiled Father Squirrel as he pointed the telescope up at the dark night sky.

Both little squirrels stood on their tiptoes and took it in turns to look at the moon through the big brass telescope.

"Can you see the Man in the Moon yet?" joked their Father.

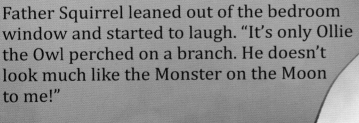

All of a sudden, the two little squirrels let go of the telescope and hid under their bed.

"There's a huge monster on the moon with great big staring eyes!" they shouted with fright.

Father Squirrel leaned out of the bedroom window and started to laugh. "It's only Ollie the Owl perched on a branch. He doesn't look much like the Monster on the Moon to me!"

Goodnight Everybody

Mrs Hedgehog had such a large family it took simply ages for her ten children to get ready for bed.

When all the little hedgehogs had been bathed, they sat together in front of a warm fire with milk and biscuits. The very last thing they did before they went to bed, was brush their teeth and comb their bristly spines. All this took a very long time!

At last, when they were all tucked up in bed and Baby Hedgehog was settled down in his wooden cot, Mrs Hedgehog would say goodnight to every one of her ten children.

Ten children, ten 'goodnights', what a long job! Then all the children would say goodnight to Mrs Hedgehog, and then say goodnight to each other!

Some nights, they would forget Baby Hedgehog, so they had to begin all over again!

"I shall never get my children to sleep," Mrs Hedgehog would sometimes sigh. However, she usually did, although it was often very late.

One night when all the little hedgehogs were fast asleep, Oswald Owl flew into a tree nearby and began to hoot very loudly. All the little hedgehogs woke up at once, got out of their beds and began to play.

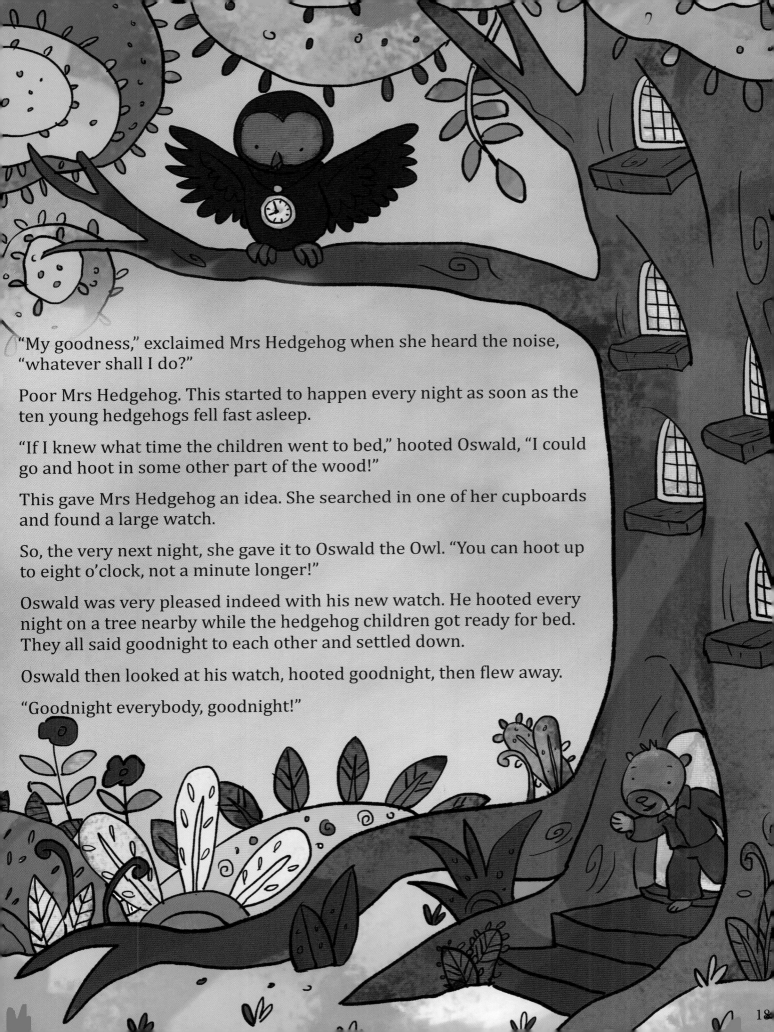

"My goodness," exclaimed Mrs Hedgehog when she heard the noise, "whatever shall I do?"

Poor Mrs Hedgehog. This started to happen every night as soon as the ten young hedgehogs fell fast asleep.

"If I knew what time the children went to bed," hooted Oswald, "I could go and hoot in some other part of the wood!"

This gave Mrs Hedgehog an idea. She searched in one of her cupboards and found a large watch.

So, the very next night, she gave it to Oswald the Owl. "You can hoot up to eight o'clock, not a minute longer!"

Oswald was very pleased indeed with his new watch. He hooted every night on a tree nearby while the hedgehog children got ready for bed. They all said goodnight to each other and settled down.

Oswald then looked at his watch, hooted goodnight, then flew away.

"Goodnight everybody, goodnight!"

Maggie Keeps Quiet

Maggie was a little girl who made a lot of noise.

You could hear her shouting all over the house and right down the road. In fact, Maggie's voice was so loud, everyone in the town could hear her.

One day her Nana sent her a present... 'The Little Hairdresser's Kit,'

Her toys were pleased. Her pets were thrilled, and her mum was delighted.

"The Little Hairdresser's Kit will keep her quiet for a while," everyone agreed.

"We can but hope!" said her dad in a whisper.

When Maggie opened her present, it was full of combs and grips and rollers and pins, as well as a pair of very safe scissors!

For the rest of that day, Maggie was totally silent. All you could hear (if you really listened hard) was the snip, snip, snip, of the very safe scissors, and the quiet pfffft, of hairspray.

"I've finished," said Maggie softly as she opened her bedroom door.

It was Mum's turn to scream! It was Dad's turn to shout! The toys and the pets made so much noise ... you could hear them all over the house, right down the road. In fact, everyone in the town could hear them!

Skip's Springs

Skip the hare had very long legs. He could hop so far and jump so high and run so fast, that no-one could keep up with him.

Nobody ever went for a walk with Skip, or jogged, or went on a cross-country run with him, because he always left everyone far behind.

So Skip sat at home all alone feeling very sorry for himself.

One day as he sat by himself, his favourite chair fell to pieces and all the springs popped out!

Did this worry Skip? Not one bit...it gave him a wonderful idea!

Now his friends have no trouble keeping up with Skip at all!

Paddy's Helpers

Paddy the Park-keeper sat down on a grassy bank in his park and mopped his brow.

"The west wind was blowing hard last night. It blew the litter baskets over and scattered paper all round my nice clean park."

And Paddy mopped his brow again.

"I've been picking up litter all day long. My back aches and I'm hot and tired!"

Now the hedgehog family happened to be playing hide and seek under the bushes. They heard what Paddy the Park-keeper said, and they felt sorry for him.

"We'll have all this paper picked up in a jiffy, and have some fun at the same time!" giggled the oldest hedgehog.

Very soon all the little hedgehogs began to roll over and over and over, squealing and laughing. The paper stuck to their prickles, and the litter in the park was cleared up in next to no time.

Paddy was delighted, the hedgehog family had a great time and were each given a strawberry ice cream as a reward!

Big Ben Comes To Help

One morning early in the summer, a long articulated lorry drove through the farmyard gate.

On the back trailer were lots of big packing cases. The Little Green Tractor wondered what they could be.

So the Little Green Tractor started up his engine and helped the lorry driver unload all those mysterious packing cases.

"I'm far too busy baling hay this morning," the farmer told his son Willie. "You'd better take a look inside!"

Now when Willie opened the first packing case, he guessed at once what was inside.

Straightaway he rang his girlfriend Tessa, who was a mechanic, and he asked her to come over as quickly as she could.

"We shall need a bit of help," said Willie to the Little Green Tractor as they rolled a giant wheel across the farmyard.

Everyone worked hard, and soon all the packing cases were empty, and the yard was full of lots of bits and pieces of an enormous machine.

It didn't take Willie and Tessa too long to put it all together, because they had a book that told you how, and lots of special spanners.

The Little Green Tractor helped too, of course!

"Well I never!" yelled the farmer from the hay field. "That's my new Giant Tractor - I quite forgot I'd ordered him!"

The Little Green Tractor looked up at the gigantic tractor in amazement.

"I'm Big Ben!" said the huge machine. "Thank you for putting me together. Will you be my best friend?"

"I'd like that," the Little Green Tractor sighed. "But I don't think the farmer will want me any more, now he has you!"

"Stuff and nonsense!" laughed the farmer. "I ordered Big Ben to help you." He patted the Little Green Tractor's bonnet. "I don't want to wear you out. I've got far too much land now for a little tractor like you."

So the Little Green Tractor was happy helping his friend Big Ben in the fields all day long.

And at night, they parked side by side in the farmer's new tractor shed.

Bathtime By The Sea

"I shan't be seeing you for a while," said Peter to his bathtime toys. "Tomorrow I am going on a week's holiday by the sea."

Then Peter dried each toy carefully on a towel, and put them back on the shelf by the side of the bath.

"That's dreadful news!" cried the toy sailor as soon as Peter had closed the bathroom door. "We shall miss seven nights of bathtime fun. It's just not fair!"

The poor bathroom toys spent a miserable night knowing that they would be left alone for a whole week.

Early next morning Peter rushed into the bathroom and scooped up his bathtime toys. He dropped them into the carrier bag, and his dad put them into the boot of his car with the rest of the luggage.

"It's a much better idea to take your toys from the bathroom on holiday," the whale and the penguin heard Peter's mum say. "Your teddy's fur would get soaking wet and full of sand, he's better left at home!"

"That means that we must be going to the seaside instead of teddy!" yelled the bathtime toys, and they hugged one another inside the carrier bag.

What a wonderful week it was. Peter took his toys down to the beach every single day.

He built a sand castle and dug a moat all the way round, then he filled the moat up with buckets of water from the sea.

Peter made the toy sailor 'King of the Castle', the penguin and the seal were guards, and the rest of the toys floated around in the moat - to save the castle from attack!

"What a great game this is!" laughed the whale. "I wish I could stay at the seaside for ever!"

That night the tide came in and washed Peter's sand castle away, but when the tide went out, it left behind rock pools full of all sorts of exciting creatures.

The rest of the holiday Peter played on the rocks while his bathtime toys explored the pools.

The seal and the whale raced and chased in and out with the rainbow-coloured fish, and the penguin made friends with a great big crab. The toy sailor went diving with the yellow ducks, and the sailing boats just bobbed up and down in the water.

"Time to go home!" said Peter at the end of the very last day.

So before they left the sea-shore the toys gathered a few of the prettiest shells to remind them of their first holiday by the sea.

Off To Camp

It was nearing the end of the long school summer holidays, and the little hedgehogs were feeling a bit bored.

"Can we go camping?" the eldest hedgehog asked his mother.

And Mrs Hedgehog agreed, that if he would take charge, they could go. So the ten little hedgehogs began to pack at once.

"We're going to camp! We're going to camp!" sang the youngest as he shoved his clothes and his books and his toys and all his bedding into a rucksack.

"I'll carry the tent!" one little hedgehog offered, but the tent was so heavy, it took four of them.

"We'll carry the pots and pans!" shouted two more.

So as soon as the ten little hedgehogs had packed everything they could possibly need, they set off to find a good place to camp.

They hadn't gone very far before Baby Hedgehog's legs felt very tired, and he asked to be carried. A little further on, the two hedgehogs carrying the pots and pans tripped over, and everything went rolling down the lane.

"Let's try to put up a tent," said the eldest one who was in charge. "Have any of you put up a tent before?" Baby Hedgehog asked, just out of interest - and nine little hedgehogs shook their heads.

They struggled and struggled all afternoon, the little hedgehogs were so busy, they had no time to stop for a meal - not even a tiny snack.

"I'm hungry," Baby Hedgehog cried. "It will be getting dark soon and I want to go home!"

Now the other little hedgehogs hadn't thought that they would be sleeping in a tent, in the dark, far away from their mum, and with no supper!

So quick as they could they packed up their things and raced for home.

Now when, at last, the ten little hedgehogs reached their garden gate it was almost dark.

"I smell fried bread," cried Baby Hedgehog. "And sausages and baked potatoes!"

"Welcome home," smiled their mother. "I thought I would camp in the garden tonight. Would you like to join me?"

And of course, they did!

Sylvester Winds The Clock

The Mayor was standing outside the town hall gazing up at the clock. He was looking very worried indeed.

"Whatever is the matter, Mr Mayor?" asked Sylvester the stork, as he strolled by with a few of his friends.

"It's the clock!" the Mayor replied, still looking up.

"Right on time!" said Sylvester looking carefully at his watch. "Four o'clock, on the dot!"

"The town hall clock is always exactly right," said the Mayor very grandly. "That isn't the problem."

"Then may I know what the problem is?" asked Sylvester the stork, polite as ever.

Suddenly the Mayor stared down at Sylvester's watch. "Sylvester," said the Mayor with a smile. "I no longer have a problem, thanks to you!" ... and Sylvester listened very carefully to what the Mayor had to say.

"I have to go away today," said the Mayor. "And I need a responsible stork with a watch, to wind the town hall clock."

Sylvester opened his beak to speak, but before he could utter one single word, the Mayor had handed over the clock key and vanished!

"How on earth am I going to get to the top of the clock tower?" cried Sylvester, very dismayed.

His friends opened their beaks to speak...

"Don't tell me!" cried Sylvester. "I need a ladder. No, I need two ladders, the clock tower is so high!"

Once again his friends opened their beaks to speak... but Sylvester had already found two ladders and was busy lashing them together with a rope.

"They're not long enough!" he wailed. "I need some scaffolding!"

Yet again his friends tried to say something...but Sylvester was in no mood to listen.

In a short while, a builder's truck drove up to the town hall carrying a load of scaffolding. Swiftly the pieces were bolted together and fitted all round the clock tower of the town hall.

"I can't climb up there!" cried poor Sylvester, and he hid his head under his wing...and his friends got a chance to speak at last...

"You silly stork!" they yelled all together. "The Mayor asked you to wind the clock, because he knew you could FLY up to the tower - and we've been trying to tell you all the time!"

Nina Puts Out The Fire

Nina's dad was a helicopter pilot. The little girl often saw him flying overhead, as she lived in a house quite new to the airfield.

Sometimes her dad would hover very low over their garden in his helicopter. Nina's dad also took her to the airfield to have a look round. There were lots of different planes on the ground, but Nina liked her dad's little helicopter best of all.

"Would you like to go up for a flight today?" her dad asked Nina.

"Yes please!" said Nina. "Can we fly over our garden and wave to Mum?"

So Nina and her dad climbed aboard and took off.

They hadn't gone very far before a call came through on the helicopter's radio.

"There's a huge grass fire on the side of the runway!" a voice said. "Our airfield fire-engine is being repaired. Can you help?"

Nina and her dad could see clouds of thick smoke rising from the airfield.

"If we don't do something quickly," said Nina's dad anxiously, "the grass fire will spread to the control tower!"

"Look down below," cried Nina. "I can see Mum in our garden!"

"We've no time to wave now!" yelled Nina's dad above the noise of the helicopter.

"Can you see my paddling pool?" shouted the little girl. "If we could hook it underneath the helicopter, and carry it across to the airfield, it might put out the fire!"

"Great idea!" nodded Nina's dad, and he hovered carefully over the garden, while Nina dropped ropes and hooks out of the helicopter door.

All the neighbours rushed outside to help and very soon the paddling pool was ready to go.

Nina's dad took his helicopter up high over the garden and flew very carefully across to the airfield.

"Let go of the ropes now!" he shouted to Nina as he hovered over the fire.

As the little girl let the ropes fall, all the water from the paddling pool dropped onto the flames.

The fire was put out at once and the control tower was safe...and Nina and her dad and the little helicopter, were given a great big cheer when they touched down!

Griselda In Charge

The farmer and his wife were planning to go away for the whole day. That meant the animals would be all alone.

"I'm rather worried about leaving Griselda," said the farmer.

"Although she's a great favourite of mine, she can be such a scatterbrain and a really silly goose sometimes."

And as the farmer's wife looked across the farmyard, we could quite see what the farmer meant.

There was Griselda, flapping her wings, cackling and squawking as she raced round and round the farmyard.

"Whatever shall we do with that silly goose?" groaned the farmer shaking his head.

"I think I know the answer!" said the farmer's wife with a little secret smile.

Very early next morning before the farmer and his wife went away for the day they woke up Griselda and said. "You're in charge today!"...and off they went.

"What me? I can't believe it! It's not true!" Griselda gabbled, running round and round in panic.

Then all of a sudden she stopped, took a deep breath, then said quite calmly,

"I AM IN CHARGE!"

Without a moment's thought, Griselda flew up onto a pile of hay and began shouting orders to the astonished animals.

"Cows, march into the milking shed!

Pigs, hoe the turnips!

Sheep, rake the hay!

Donkey, take the milk to market!

Dog, drive the tractor!"

Griselda the goose wasn't finished yet, there were lots more orders to come.

"Goats, mend the barn roof!

Cats, tidy up the farmyard!

Turkey, pump the water!

And chickens, chop the firewood!"

When, at last, the farmer and his wife returned, they couldn't believe how much work had been done.

"What a sensible goose you've turned out to be!" said the farmer as he patted Griselda on the head.

"I just knew she would!" smiled the farmer's wife.

"It's very hard being in charge," cackled Griselda, flapping her wings and racing round and round the farmyard. "I'd much rather be silly!"

And the farmer and his wife just shook their heads and sighed...

Mr Fox Plays Statue

Have you ever played the statue game? - It's great fun!

...One person turns their back while everyone else runs about, and when that

his garden. "Bobby Rabbit and his horrid little pals will never get my strawberries!"

What Mr Fox didn't know, was that Bobby Rabbit and his friends were hiding behind

person turns around, everybody must keep perfectly still - just like a statue!

If you as much as blink, you are out! And the person who keeps still the longest is the winner.

Bobby Rabbit and his friends loved playing statues, and one day they used their favourite game to trick crafty Mr Fox.

It happened in early summer.

Right in the middle of Mr Fox's garden was a big bed of ripe juicy strawberries.

"I shall keep watch day and night," said Mr Fox out loud, as he stood on guard in

his garden shed. They were all holding empty baskets - just waiting to fill them with all those lovely ripe strawberries.

"Good afternoon, Mr Fox." called Bobby Rabbit. "I've never seen anyone stand so perfectly still! Can you play statues?"

"No-one is better at standing still than me," boasted Mr Fox. "And I'm brilliant at playing statues!"

"Would you show us how to play?" begged Bobby Rabbit trying hard not to giggle.

So Mr Fox left his strawberry patch, and went over to show Bobby Rabbit and his friends how to play the statue game.

"He's so good at it," sighed Bobby Rabbit, and he gazed at Mr Fox standing perfectly still.

As the game went on, the little animals crept away, one by one.

Quietly they sneaked into Mr Fox's strawberry patch, filled up their baskets then scurried off home.

At last the game came to an end, and Mr Fox was the only one left standing in the garden as still as a statue!

Now Bobby Rabbit should have told Mr Fox that he was the winner, but that crafty rabbit's mouth was too full of strawberries!

The Striped Submarine

The Striped Submarine always felt a bit sleepy in the afternoon, so most days she had a little nap and drifted drowsily just beneath the waves.

"I must have been asleep for hours," said the Striped Submarine.

"It's got dark while I've been dreaming."

"No, it's not dark yet," laughed a passing jelly-fish. "A silly seagull has built her nest on top of your periscope!"

"Oh no!" gasped the Striped Submarine. "She'll have to find somewhere else, or I won't be able to dive down deep below the water!"

"I'm dreadfully sorry," cackled the silly seagull. "I've already laid three eggs, so I shall have to stay here until my chicks hatch and are big enough to fly away!"

"How long will that take?" asked the Striped Submarine, very shocked indeed.

"At least twelve weeks!" said the silly seagull.

The Striped Submarine heaved a great big sigh, and almost dived down to the bottom of the sea.

"Try to remember," the jelly-fish told the submarine, "you can go up but not down!"

So for twelve whole weeks, the Striped Submarine cruised round and round the ocean, with the silly seagull and her three chicks on top of her periscope.

As you can see, the ocean folks made quite sure she wasn't ever bored or lonely. And when the seagull chicks grew big and flew away - the Striped Submarine really missed them!

202

Belinda's Super-Duper Ice-Cream

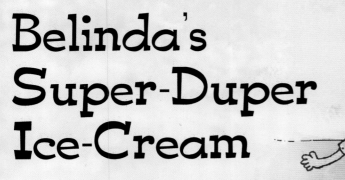

It was the middle of the summer. The sun was blazing down from a clear blue sky making all the toys feel hot and tired. Even the toy soldier had changed into shorts and tee-shirt.

"Why don't you take your coat off?" the toy soldier asked Belinda the rag-doll.

"You know I hardly ever do that!" she snapped back, (really, Belinda was beginning to feel hot and tired too). "I shall have an ice-cream to keep cool!" Off she went to fetch one.

Now when Belinda returned, she was holding the biggest ice-cream you ever did see, but that selfish ragdoll couldn't be bothered to bring any ices back for the other toys.

"I shall eat my super-duper ice cream in a moment" said Belinda taking a deep breath. "But first I shall tell you all about it!" ...and she did.

"My super-duper ice-cream tastes of... strawberry and vanilla and fudge and toffee and butterscotch sauce with double chocolate chips and jelly beans on top!"

Sad to say, Belinda was so busy talking that her super-duper ice-cream melted away in the hot sun. It ran the whole way down her best coat and splashed onto her new shoes!

"Serves you right for being so selfish," laughed the toy soldier, and he rushed off to buy everyone an ice cream.

As for Belinda - she spent the rest of that hot afternoon cleaning her best coat and new shoes!

Two Brave Little Astronauts

Two brave little astronauts went off to the Moon in a shiny silver rocket.

They both wore special space suits with lots of useful zips and pockets.

They had helmets on their heads and air-packs on their backs, and on their feet were absolutely enormous moon-boots.

As soon as they landed on the Moon, the two brave little astronauts walked all over the surface, and left very, very big footprints with their absolutely enormous moon-boots.

One of them whizzed off in the moon buggy while the other one gathered a bucketful of moon dust.

Then before they left for home one of them planted a flag to prove that the two brave little astronauts had really been to the moon.

"Time to go home!" said one to the other. So they headed back to Earth without delay.

At last they returned and splashed down safely in the sea.

One of the brave little astronauts opened the hatch to wave his flag and shout, "Hurrah!"

"Where did you get that flag?" asked the other.

"Some careless person left it on the Moon. I thought it made the place look untidy... so I brought it home!"

Emmy's Big Toe

Emmy the elephant hurt her big toe. She tripped over and banged it as she ran to get her breakfast.

"You great big silly!" cried Norah, the zoo-keeper's wife, as she served breakfast to the other animals.

"Ouch!" yelled Emmy, between mouthfuls of hot buttered toast. "Ouch, ouch, ouch!"

"Where does it hurt?" asked Norah kindly.

"My big toe!" Emmy yelled as she munched an extra slice.

"There, there!" said Norah. "We'd better let the vet take a look at you. "And off she went to telephone him.

"Ouch!" yelled Emmy once again. The other animals felt sorry for her, so they made her lots more toast - just to make her feel better.

When the vet arrived to examine Emmy's big toe, he opened his black bag and took out a sticking plaster.

"Will it hurt?" Emmy gasped, still munching toast.

"Not a bit," the vet replied as he stuck on the plaster. "Rest that big toe for at least a week, young lady!" And off he went.

"Now that could be a bit of a problem," sighed Norah. "I don't think we have a wheel-chair big enough for you, Emmy!"

"I can't stay in the same place for a whole week!" wailed Emmy who by now had eaten every bit of the breakfast toast.

It wasn't long before the zookeeper came across to find out what had happened. He had heard Emmy shouting, "Ouch, ouch, ouch!" and wondered what was going on.

"She needs to rest her big toe!" said Norah. "Whatever are we going to do?"

"No problem at all!" cried the zoo-keeper, and off he went to telephone a factory nearby.

All the zoo animals stayed with Emmy to keep her company. Every so often she would shout, "Ouch, ouch, ouch!" Just to remind them that her big toe still hurt.

"It's arrived! It's arrived!" shouted the zoo-keeper as a lorry reversed carefully through the gates of the zoo.

There on the back, waiting to be unloaded...was a fork-lift truck!

"Perfect!" cried Norah quite delighted. "It's just the thing for taking Emmy round the zoo for a week!"

Norman The Nervous Ghost Train

Have you ever been on a Ghost Train? I have, and it's very scary.

This is the story of Norman the Nervous Ghost Train, who took children on a spooky ride at the fair.

Every day Norman carried passengers through long dark eerie tunnels, on a spine-chilling, nail-biting trip, where monsters spring out in front, skeletons rattle their bones all around, and big black hairy spiders dangle from the ceiling, and silky cobwebs brush your face, and make everyone scream and shriek!

"Isn't this fun!" cried one little boy who often went for a ride on the Nervous Ghost Train.

"Not one bit!" replied Norman shaking with fright "I'll never get used to all those scary things inside that dark tunnel."

This made the little boy laugh out loud. "It's just pretend. The monsters aren't real. The ghosts are old white sheets and the spiders are bits of fur on string!"

"It's still very scary," mumbled the nervous Ghost Train feeling very embarrassed.

"You need a holiday with some fresh air and sunshine!" said the little boy.

"Come with me to the country, and I promise you'll feel a lot better."

So the little boy drove the Nervous Ghost Train out of the fairground and never stopped until they reached the green fields and hills of the countryside.

As they sped along, they passed a field full of black and white cows.

"MOO! MOO! MOO!" they bellowed, and scattered in all directions.

It wasn't long before the Nervous Ghost Train gave a flock of sheep a terrible fright. They ran away as fast as they could, so did the rabbits and the pigs and all the fowls in the farmyard.

"Whatever is the matter with all the animals?" asked the nervous Ghost Train. "Who is making them so frightened?"

"You are!" smiled the little boy. "They've never seen a ghost train before."

"But they needn't be frightened of me," laughed Norman.

"And you shouldn't be frightened of those pretend monsters and skeletons and hairy spiders at the fairground!"

The Nervous Ghost Train looked down at the ground. "I have been a bit silly," he mumbled.

"I should say so!" said the little boy. "You must come to the countryside more often. The animals will soon get used to you."

"I could give them all a ride," suggested the Nervous Ghost Train- and he did!

After a while the little boy drove Norman back to the fairground, where a long queue of children stood waiting for a ride.

"Jump aboard," puffed the Nervous Ghost Train, "for the scariest ride of your lives!" This made the children shriek and scream at the tops of their voices!

"Watch out ghosts, skeletons and monsters, big hairy spiders and dangling cobwebs ... HERE I COME!"

Then Norman the Nervous Ghost Train gave the little boy a great big wink, then disappeared into the long dark tunnel.

Don't Say Cuckoo!

When Mum read the children a bedtime story all the toys loved to listen.

"I do wish story-time could go on a bit longer," said one of the children.

"So do we!" whispered the toys very quietly.

"When the cuckoo clock on the wall says it's eight o'clock, I must close the storybook because it's bedtime," said Mum.

"Even if you haven't finished the story?" cried one of the children.

"I'm afraid so," said Mum quite firmly.

"One of us ought to have a word with that cuckoo clock," said the toy panda. "But I'm far too big and heavy to climb up there!"

So a few of the smaller and lighter toys decided to try.

At last they reached the cuckoo clock and knocked on the little door.

The cuckoo inside was delighted to meet them and said he would love to help. He agreed to keep quiet at eight o'clock (for a little while at least!).

"Your bedtime stories seem to take longer every night," said Mum as she carried on reading, but everyone was too busy listening to reply...especially the cuckoo in the clock on the wall!

209

Big Bear's New Bed

"I need a new bed!" said Big Bear one morning. "My head sticks out the top, and my toes out the bottom, and I'm afraid if I turn over during the night I shall fall out of bed onto the floor!"

And as Big Bear turned over, just to show the others what he meant, he rolled off the bed and landed on the floor with a thump.

This made the little bears laugh so much, they had to have several glasses of water to help them calm down!

"Why don't you leave it to us, Big Bear?" cried the little bears after breakfast. "We'll go and see the Bear Who Makes Furniture. He'll make a bed big enough for you!"

"How big is he?" asked the Bear Who Makes Furniture.

"He's as big as this!" said one little bear, stretching out his arms as wide as he could.

"He's much bigger than that!" argued the other little bears. "He's absolutely enormous!"

"He's at least as big as this!" cried three more of the little bears as they joined paws to form a circle.

"He must be a giant bear then!" gasped the Bear Who Makes Furniture.

At last the bed was finished. It took several of the strongest bears to carry it over to Big Bear's house.

"It's big enough for everyone!" joked Big Bear when he saw his brand new bed.

"Wonderful!" cried the little bears as they jumped up and down. "Now we can all share one great bed. Won't that be fun?"

...but Big Bear doesn't look too sure, does he?...

Mr Wolf's Big Sister

One day the three little pigs were strolling down the lane, when Mr Wolf came running by.

He didn't even notice the three little pigs, which was very strange, because he was always trying to catch them and gobble them up!

So the three little pigs followed Mr Wolf to find out what was going on.

At the bottom of the lane they spied him waiting at the bus stop.

"Perhaps Mr Wolf is going away, and he'll never bother us again!" said one little pig.

"No such luck!" moaned the other two.

Then along came the bus, and when it stopped Mr Wollf's big sister stepped off.

"She looks very fierce, just look at those teeth!" gasped the first little pig.

"She looks very strong, just look at those claws!" gasped the second little pig.

"She looks fine to me!" said the third little pig. "Shall I go over and say 'Hello'!"

"Indeed you will not!" the other two pigs cried. "Let's run home before they gobble up the lot of us!"

When they were safe inside the three little pigs sat down to think.

"Three little pigs like us are no match for Mr Wolf and his big sister," they agreed. "We'll have to think up a daring plan!" And so they did.

The very next morning the three little pigs went over to Mr Wolf's house and knocked on his door.

One little pig was carrying a beautiful bunch of flowers. One had a big box of chocolates tied with a red ribbon, the other little pig was holding a huge basket of fruit.

"These gifts are for your beautiful big sister!" said the three little pigs grinning broadly (although their knees were knocking together loudly).

Now Mr Wolf was just about to grab hold of them, when his big sister stepped outside.

"For me?" she sighed, and she tickled each little pig on the nose.

Then she opened her chocolates and shared them with the three little pigs... and what is more... she made Mr Wolf do all the little pig's chores!

He mended the roof and painted the fence. He chopped enough firewood for a whole winter. He mowed the lawn and cut the hedge - he even swept the chimney!

"It's my way of saying 'Thank you' to these three sweet, kind and charming little pigs!" said Mr Wolf's big sister.

The New School

Minnie and Winnie had just moved house. They liked their new home. There was plenty of space and a big garden - so why did the girls look so glum?

Mrs Morris, their new neighbour, popped her head over the wall.

"Pleased to meet you, girls!" she called. "You both look as if you need cheering up."

"I do!" sighed Minnie, and she folded her arms.

"Me too!" agreed Winnie, and she did the same.

So Mrs Morris came into the garden to see what she could do.

"We start our new school tomorrow," said both girls together. "And we don't want to go. Not ever!"

Mrs Morris stepped back in amazement. "Is that the big school across the park, with playing fields all around?"

The twins nodded, still looking very glum.

"Is that the school that has hamsters and gerbils and fluffy baby rabbits, with a fish-pond and a bird table in the garden?"

"We think so," said the girls looking interested. "Is that the school where they bake cakes and go swimming, and have picnics in the summer and parties at Christmas time?"

"We hope so, Mrs Morris!" and the twins ran inside to get ready for school in the morning.

Next day Minnie and Winnie could not wait to get to school.

As they opened their classroom door, they heard a familiar voice say, "Welcome Minnie and Winnie. I'm your new teacher, Mrs Morris!"

Don't Open The Box

Helen the hamster was very inquisitive. She often poked her little pink nose where it wasn't wanted.

"I'm just curious!" said Helen as she tried all the perfumes and powders on someone else's dressing table.

"Do try not to be so nosey!" complained one of Helen's friends as the little hamster peered into all her kitchen cupboards.

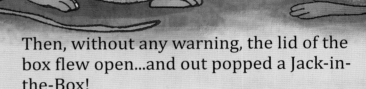

Now one day, Helen the hamster found a mysterious wooden box on the floor.

"I must find out what's inside!" said Helen as she tried to lift the lid.

"It's locked!"she cried, and that made the little hamster more curious than ever.

"I'm sure I can guess where the key is!" Of course inquisitive Helen found it straight away.

"Someone doesn't want me to know what's inside the box!" sniggered Helen, and she turned the key.

As she did, a strange whirring-sound seemed to come from inside the box.

"It's a music box," Helen smiled. "I knew it all the time!"

Then, without any warning, the lid of the box flew open...and out popped a Jack-in-the-Box!

He gave poor Helen the fright of her life.

"Serves you right!" he cackled. "That's what you get for being nosey!".

The Haunted Glade

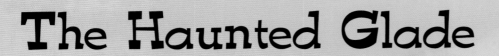

Messenger Mole delivered the mail all around the wood. His aunt, Miss Mole, sorted out the letters for every animal that lived in the woodland.

"How very odd," remarked Miss Mole, one day, "They're all the same!"

It took Messenger Mole all morning to deliver the letters, and by lunchtime he was quite exhausted.

His last call was at the house of Mr Grey Badger.

"Let's open our letters together," suggested Messenger Mole to the badger. "Mine's an invitation to a party at midnight in the Haunted Glade deep in the wood!"

"So is mine," said Mr Grey Badger waving his letter in the air. "It looks very suspicious to me!"

"Nonsense!" cried Messenger Mole. "I'm going!" And off he scuttled.

All that day the animals showed one another their party invitations - they were all the same!

"I don't like going anywhere near the Haunted Glade," whispered Miss Mole, "It's so dark and spooky!"

"Nonsense!" said Messenger Mole. "We'll all go together and carry lanterns. It would be a shame to miss a party."

"Sounds like fun to me," squeaked Mildred Mouse.

So the woodland animals busied about all the rest of that day, looking for their party clothes and ironing out the creases wherever necessary.

Only Mr Grey Badger decided to stay at home. "Don't know what all the fuss is about," he muttered to anyone who would listen. "I think it's very suspicious inviting us all to visit the Haunted Glade at midnight." A strange look came over his face. "I shall go indoors and do some thinking!"

Once it grew dark, the animals changed into their party clothes and waited.

"It seems an awfully long time to midnight," said Mildred Mouse, who was having a hard time keeping her little ones awake.

Mrs Grey Rabbit, on the other hand, had put all her bunnies to bed at six o'clock, and promised she would wake them at

eleven, in time to get ready and reach the Haunted Glade by midnight.

At last it was almost time. Small groups of animals carrying torches and lamps gathered outside their front doors.

"Are you sure you won't join us and come to the party?" asked Messenger Mole as he passed Mr Grey Badger's house.

"No!" replied Badger, who was dressed up in a dark hat and overcoat and carrying his cricket bat. "I've got work to do!"

"At midnight?" thought Messenger Mole who quickly forgot all about Badger and joined Mildred Mouse and several others who were heading for the Haunted Glade.

It was a very long walk in the dark and cold.

"Is the Haunted Glade really haunted?" asked one little rabbit.

"Listen!" whispered a fox cub. "I think I can hear ghosts moaning and groaning!" This made all the young animals shake with fright.

"Stop being so silly!" snapped Mrs Grey Rabbit. "We've been invited to a party, so let's get a move on, it's almost twelve o'clock."

"Ghosts come out on the stroke of midnight!" said a little rabbit in a trembling voice.

"Now that's just silly!" his mother replied.

At long last they reached the Haunted Glade...and what do you think they found...NOTHING...no lights, no party food or balloons and no music for dancing - in fact the Haunted Glade was completely empty.

"I think we've been tricked," said Mrs Grey Rabbit. "There's no party at all!"

Slowly the animals trudged back to their homes in the familiar part of the wood... And there was Mr Grey Badger waiting to welcome them home.

"We've all been tricked!" said Messenger Mole quietly.

"You certainly have!" Mr Badger replied, as a broad grin spread across his face, which made the animals feel even more embarrassed.

"I thought there was something very odd about those invitations," said Badger beginning to enjoy himself.

"So I stayed here to see what would happen, and my suspicions were quite correct."

"Do tell us what happened!" begged Messenger Mole as he tugged at Badger's overcoat.

"This is what happened!"and he switched on a powerful light outside his front door.

There, in a heap on the ground, were two wicked stoats and an evil weasel. They were tied up with ropes and gagged with several of Miss Mole's best scarves,

and scattered all around were some of the woodland creatures' most treasured possessions.

"You've been burgled!" announced Badger, grabbing one of the stoats by the scruff of the neck and holding him up high.

Everyone gasped!

"While you were away at this so called party, these three no-good fellows broke into your houses and stole everything," went on Mr Badger.

"Then those party invitations I delivered were nothing but a trick!" cried poor Messenger Mole.

"Absolutely!" said Badger. "It's lucky I stayed behind!"

"Very lucky!" cried Mildred Mouse and Mrs Grey Rabbit, and they rushed forward to give Badger a hug and a kiss.

"Steady on!" said Badger blushing. "Now off to bed everyone.

You must all be very tired - especially the little ones. I shall lock these three fellows in my cellar and deal with them in the morning."

So the tired woodland animals picked up all their treasures that had been stolen and stumbled off to bed.

"It's a good job we've got a clever chap like you to look after us, Badger," said Messenger Mole as he rubbed his eyes.

"It certainly is!" agreed Mr Badger as he handed the mole a cup of strong tea.

"Tomorrow afternoon, at three o'clock sharp, I shall give a party.

There'll be fancy cakes and salad sandwiches, and we'll have games with prizes and music for dancing!" announced Badger as he poured himself some more tea.

"Messenger Mole! Will you take out the invitations first thing in the morning?" ...but Messenger Mole was already fast asleep.

Balloons Everywhere

Lewis went to a wedding. At the party afterwards there were lots and lots of lovely balloons.

They were tied to all the tables and chairs with bright shiny ribbons...big balloons, little balloons, and very special balloons that scattered pretty confetti all over the room when they went POP!

Lewis and the rest of the children at the wedding had a wonderful time with so many balloons to play with.

They raced and chased round and round until they were tired out.

Then one by one they sat down with a FLOP, and let go of their balloons... What do you think happened? ...

...One by one the balloons floated up to the ceiling and stayed there.

The children were most upset - except one!

Lewis had noticed the balloons fixed to the tables and chairs. So when he wanted to jump about and have fun, he tied his balloons to his wrist and some round his middle.

Clever boy, Lewis! But be careful you don't float up to the ceiling and stay there!

Vera Takes A Shower

Vera the viper was very vain. She simply could not stop admiring herself.

"I look so pretty," Vera said as she passed a puddle. "No, I'm wrong!"sighed the vain viper as she gazed at her own reflection, "I look absolutely beautiful!"

Now the garden was very damp that morning, so Vera spent lots of time admiring herself as she went from puddle to puddle.

Then all at once, as she slithered along, Vera came across another snake.

"How plain she looks!" hissed Vera rudely. "How skinny and how boring!"

Then without any warning, a shower of icy water hit Vera in the face.

"What a nasty-tempered snake!" gasped poor Vera, soaking wet and very cold.

Little did Vera know, she had been talking to the GARDEN HOSE.

Emilio's Present

It was Emilio's birthday. The little Mexican boy had been given lots of presents and he felt very happy.

"There is one more very special gift," said Emilio's father. "But first you must promise that you will look after it always."

So Emilio promised, then ran off to find his very special birthday present.

As Emilio ran round the side of the house he could hardly believe his eyes. For there, standing in the middle of the yard, was his very own little donkey.

"I shall call you 'Paco'!" said Emilio as he led his new friend across the yard for a cool drink.

Now Paco was far too small to reach the water trough, but the little Mexican boy soon solved the problem.

"I promised to look after you always," laughed Emilio. "And I will!"

Nipper's New Wheels

One dreadful day, Nipper the pull-along dog lost his wheels! One by one they fell off and vanished without trace in the garden.

"Poor Nipper!" said the toy robot. "What are you going to do?"

"Not a lot!" replied Nipper sadly. "Without my wheels, I could stay in the same place for ever!"

"Let's take a good look round," suggested the red-haired clown. "We might find something that's the same shape as your lost wheels."

So the toys began to search at once.

It wasn't long before one of them discovered a bag of big chocolate coins that belonged to the children.

"They're just perfect!" cried the red-haired clown, and with a bit of help he fixed them onto Nipper.

The chocolate wheels worked quite well for a while, until the front ones melted when the sun shone through the window, and the pet gerbil nibbled the back ones.

"Perhaps we could find some spare wheels at the bottom of the old toy chest," said the robot. "It's full of bits and pieces!"

So with a bit of effort, the toys tipped up the chest and began to search at once.

"Look what I've found!" cried one of the toys, holding up a forgotten treasure.

"I've found the trophy I won last year!" yelled the model racing driver.

"And here's the sheep-dog from the toy farm!" smiled Angie the peg doll.

"Everybody's found something they've liked or lost," said Nipper looking very disappointed. "But I can't seem to find any wheels that will fit me!"

Then suddenly, out of the old toy chest, rolled a bright yellow roller-skate.

"I'm the only one left of the pair," said the skate as he introduced himself to Nipper. "I'm no good on my own, but my wheels are just right for you!"

So the toys lifted Nipper on top of the skate, and he fitted perfectly.

"I'm even better than before!" laughed Nipper as he whizzed round the floor.

"It's my super-fast wheels!" cried the roller-skate happily...he'd been left alone and forgotten for far too long!

"I didn't know this was in here," shouted another.

"I've never seen so much rubbish," poor Nipper sighed as he gazed at all the different spare wheels ...

...There were bike wheels, pram wheels, all sorts of steering wheels, gear wheels and car wheels and every different size of wheel...but not one of the wheels would fit Nipper the pull-along dog.

"Look here!" cried a delighted doll. "I've found my old necklace and my red belt. I thought they'd gone for ever!" So she put them on straight away.

"Here's my key!" said the clockwork ladybird. "Will someone wind me up?"

Ziggie Wanders Off

All day long, Ziggie the little zebra munched sweet green grass on the big open plains of Africa.

Now Ziggie, as a rule, did as he was told and stayed close by his mother.

But one very hot afternoon, Ziggie felt so thirsty, he wandered off all by himself in search of a drink.

In a short while he came to a lake, and as he bent down and opened his mouth for a drink, another little zebra did too!

Ziggie tossed his head, and so did the other little zebra.

Ziggie wiggled his ears, and the other little zebra did the same.

"Stop copying me!" shouted Ziggie, but the other little zebra just stared back.

Then came a lot of giggling and laughing, and all the young animals standing around were very amused...

"Your new zebra friend can't speak back," giggled a baby hippo.

"You've been talking to your own reflection, Ziggie!" The little animals burst out laughing once more.

"Don't worry!" smiled a young giraffe. "We've all made the same mistake. Lots of us come to drink at this lake twice a day, so you need never be short of new friends!

Dad Phones Home

Dolly, Polly and Molly were always talking on the telephone. They rang their friends and their friends rang them back and they chattered for hours and hours.

The three girls made phone calls about swimming arrangements and dancing lessons and parties.

They rang the cinema and the theatre, the railway station and the store.

They talked to the doctor, the dentist, the vet and the hairdresser...poor Dad was never able to use the phone at all!

Then one day, Dolly, Polly and Molly looked out of the window, and there was Dad making a phone call from his very own phone box...in the garden!

Snarl Please!

Tiny Tiger Tim thought that he would take his new camera into the jungle with him.

"I shall take photographs of all the fierce and dangerous animals that live there!" he said. "When I find any of them snarling or snapping or grinding their teeth - I shall take a photo at once!"

So Tiny Tiger Tim put a film in his camera, popped his shady hat on his head and set off.

He hadn't gone very far into the steaming hot jungle when he met a leopard...all teeth and claws!

"Snarl please," said Tiny Tiger Tim as he pointed at his camera.

"So sorry," said the leopard. "I'm busy taking a shower - got to smell fresh, goodbye!"

Next Tiny Tiger Tim came upon an orang-utan sitting in the trees...he was an ugly fellow!

"Look nasty for the camera," said Tiny Tiger Tim.

"No time today," the orang-utan smiled.

"I have to practise my flute - I have an exam tomorrow!"

So Tiny Tiger Tim went on his way. Suddenly he spied a boa constrictor hanging from a branch.

"Hiss if you please," said Tiny Tiger Tim as he pointed his camera.

"Not a chance!" replied the snake as he grasped his feather duster tightly. "I'm busy cleaning my bedroom. Please go away, unless you like dusting!"

So Tiny Tiger Tim walked on through the undergrowth until he came to a crocodile.

"Give us a grin and show us those razor-sharp teeth!" Tiny Tiger Tim joked as he focused his lens.

"Not now..." said the Crocodile. "I'm just getting ready for lunch. Want to taste these delicious sandwiches I've made?"

Tiny Tiger Tim shook his head and moved on ... The crocodile looked far too ordinary with a big white napkin tucked under his chin! All of a sudden a parrot squawked loudly overhead. Crashing through the undergrowth came one of the most fierce and bad-tempered creatures of the jungle - a huge two horned rhinoceros. Straight away Tiny Tiger Tim was ready with his camera.

"How lovely to see you!" giggled the rhino with delight. "I need a little help with my lines for tomorrow night's show. It's called Jungle Jingles, and I'm the funny comedian!"

"I don't believe it," cried Tiny Tiger Tim as he glanced around.

"Jungle animals are supposed to be fierce and frightening!" yelled Tiny Tiger Tim at the top of his voice. Then he put down his camera and he roared and roared and roared!

He made so much noise that everyone from miles around came to take photographs of THE FIERCEST TIGER IN THE JUNGLE!

The Fat Ginger Cat

"I wish we could do something about that Fat Ginger Cat!" whispered the mice as Ginger stuck his head through the cat-flap.

Quickly the mice ran away into the bushes before they were caught.

"He's everywhere!" complained a brown mouse.

"We can't get into the kitchen to eat up the cake crumbs and cheesy biscuits," said another.

"It's as bad in the garden," sobbed a pretty little mouse with a pink bow. "We should be eating picnic food and tasty treats from the barbecue, but that Fat Ginger Cat gobbles up everything in sight!"

"He'll gobble you up too," called a Robin as he flew by. "Be careful! Be careful!"

"The robin is right," said the brown mouse. "Something must be done about that Fat Ginger Cat!"

Just at that moment, a dark shadow passed overhead.

"Nothing to worry about," called the brown mouse to everyone. "It's only a hot-air balloon!"

In the next few minutes giant balloons of all shapes and sizes floated across the sky.

"Aren't they beautiful?" sighed the pretty little mouse with the pink bow.

"They certainly are," agreed the brown mouse. "Now, these hot-air balloons have given me a brilliant idea!"

The Fat Ginger Cat never noticed the giant Balloons as they drifted by, he was fast asleep snoring in the warm sun.

"I need six of the strongest mice straight away!" announced the brown mouse, looking very serious.

"We are going to buy a balloon!"

After what seemed a very long time, the six strong mice came back with a large parcel and a huge ball of string.

The brown mouse unwrapped the parcel.

"Start pumping!" he cried, and the six strong mice did just that.

"Whatever is it?" asked the pretty little mouse with the pink bow.

"It's a very special Balloon that will scare the wits out of that Fat Ginger Cat!" the brown mouse sniggered.

"It's a GIANT MOUSE!" squeaked the pretty little mouse with the pink bow. "And it's even bigger than that Fat Ginger Cat!"

As the giant mouse slowly rose into the air, the Fat Ginger Cat, who was still asleep in the sun, lazily opened one eye.

The great balloon gave him such a fright, he jumped up with all four paws in the air.

"I'll never chase mice again as long as I live!" screeched the Fat Ginger Cat, and he dived into the bushes.

How the mice cheered and cheered, they were safe at last from that Fat Ginger Cat.

Elvis And The White Bear Cubs

Elvis the Eskimo heard a strange scratching and snuffling noise. It seemed to be coming from outside his igloo.

"It must be visitors," said Elvis, "and they can't find my doorbell!"

So straight away he put on his warm clothes and stepped outside to see who it could be.

"We're lost!" said a couple of tiny voices. Two polar bear cubs were huddled together behind the igloo.

"I'm not surprised," joked Elvis. "I can hardly see you myself in the white snow!"

Just at that moment Mother Bear came lumbering across the ice.

"I can never find these two!"she grumbled. "As soon as I let them go out to play, they vanish into thin air!"

"I can quite believe that," agreed Elvis as the huge polar bear towered above him.

Now the two little bear cubs were as white as the snow around them, but Elvis knew exactly how to solve their mother's problem.

He went inside his igloo and very soon came out with two brightly coloured track-suits.

"I wore these when I was small, and my mum could always find me!"

Straight away the two little bear cubs pulled on their new clothes.

"Let's play hide and seek!" they yelled as they ran off into the snow.

"I don't think so!" chuckled Mother Bear and Elvis the Eskimo.

Quack, Quack, Mr Fox

Bobby Rabbit was looking in a drawer one day when he came across a strange kind of whistle.

He took a deep breath and blew down the hole in the top with all his might.

"Quack, quack!" came the sound. "Quack, quack!"

"It's not a whistle at all!" laughed Bobby Rabbit. "It's a duck call!"

And he blew hard again. "Quack, quack! Quack, quack!"

"I could have some fun with this," Bobby Rabbit giggled, and he ran down the road to Mr Fox's house, and hid behind the hedge.

Now when Bobby Rabbit saw Mr Fox open his back door, he took out the duck-call and blew as hard as he could.

"Quack, quack! Quack, quack!"

"Do I hear a duck?" asked Mr Fox listening very hard. "Yes I do! Yes I do!" And he jumped up and down in excitement.

Straightaway Mr Fox rushed indoors. He lit his stove and put a huge pan of water to boil on the top.

"I shall have tasty roast duck with green beans and carrots for dinner tonight!" he sang at the top of his voice.

Now Bobby Rabbit, who was still hiding behind the hedge, laughed so much he could hardly blow down the duck-call.

Suddenly Mr Fox rushed out of his house. "I can't hear the duck," he gasped, looking very worried. "I hope it hasn't flown away!"

So Bobby Rabbit stopped giggling and blew on the duck-call at once.

"Quack, quack! Quack, quack!" "Splendid, splendid!" cried Mr Fox. "Duck for my dinner. What a treat!"

While he was outside listening to the duck quacking, Mr Fox picked up a bunch of carrots and a basket of green beans from his vegetable plot.

"My favourites!" whispered Bobby Rabbit from behind the hedge.

"Quack, quack! Quack, quack!"

At last the time came for Mr Fox to go behind the hedge and catch the duck for his dinner.

What a shock he got when he found Bobby Rabbit sitting there, blowing his duck-call.

"Quack, quack! Quack, quack!" Mr Fox was so angry that he threw down his basket of vegetables and had a temper-tantrum on the spot!

Quick as a flash, Bobby Rabbit grabbed the vegetables and ran for his life.

"Green beans and fresh carrots - my favourites!" he yelled as he ran home.

"Quack, quack! Quack, quack!"

The Rabbits Bedtime Story

It was getting late and almost time for the little grey rabbits to go to bed.

"Just time for a short story before I say goodnight," said their mother. So she sat down in her chair, picked up a storybook and reached inside her bag for her glasses.

"Oh dear!" said Mrs Grey Rabbit. "My bag is so full of all sorts of things, my glasses must have slipped right down to the bottom!"

First, she pulled out a packet of candy-canes, one for each of her little rabbits to nibble.

Next she found six odd socks then a golf club and a beach ball.

"I seem to have collected an awful lot of rubbish!" laughed Mrs Grey Rabbit as she pulled a mouth organ from her bag, and an old fishing-net and a seaside spade.

By now Mrs Grey Rabbit had almost reached the bottom of her bag.

"No sign of my glasses, I'm afraid!" and she pulled out the very last object - an alarm clock that began to ring very loudly.

"Oh my goodness!" gasped Mrs Grey Rabbit. "It's eight o'clock. Time all of you were in bed!"

"But we haven't had our bedtime story yet!" cried the little grey rabbits all at once.

"And I still haven't found my glasses!" said their mother shaking her head.

So the little grey rabbits began searching the room as fast as they could...in cupboards and drawers, under tables and on top of cupboards, behind the curtains and up the chimney. They even looked under the floorboards!

All of a sudden the youngest rabbit leapt into the air. "I've found them! I've found them!" he cried, and in his paw were Mother Rabbit's lost glasses.

"They were down the side of her chair all the time!" shrieked the baby rabbit.

"Gather round quickly," said Mrs Grey Rabbit popping her glasses on the end of her nose. "We've just got time for one short-story...

Once upon a time there lived a beautiful young girl and her name was Cinderella. One night she went to a ball in a great palace and she lost her glass slipper... "

Every one of the little rabbits listened quietly right to the very end of the story - except baby rabbit, who had fallen asleep at the beginning!

Wake Up Lucille

Lucille the lop-eared rabbit was always late.

She was late getting up in the morning, she was late for lunch - and at the end of the day, when bedtime came - she was late for that too!

"Tomorrow we are going on holiday together," one of her friends told Lucille that night as she got ready for bed.

"My case is packed, I've cleaned my shoes, and my clothes are all ready for tomorrow," said Lucille as she busied about checking all her clocks and watches.

"Up at six o'clock sharp!" she muttered as she set her alarm clock.

"I won't be late! I won't be late!"

Now as you may have noticed, Lucille's ears are very long. So most of the time she never hears her alarm clock ring - although it makes a very loud noise.

"How can I make really sure that I'll get up at six o'clock in the morning?" said the rabbit as she gazed around the room.

"I've got it!" shouted Lucille. "I'll sleep in the grandfather clock, then I'll be sure to hear the clock strike six, and I won't be late for my holiday!"

Peter's Present

Peter was looking for a present. "It's my brother's birthday tomorrow," he told the lady in the shop, "so I must find a present today!"

"How about some brown socks?" asked the lady.

"Too boring!" replied Peter.

"A white cotton shirt?" She held one up.

"Too plain!" Peter said, shaking his head.

"A box of handkerchiefs?" suggested the lady.

"Far too dull!" said Peter, and he thanked her and walked away.

Now as Peter strolled through the store wondering what to buy, he passed by the kitchen department. All around him he saw frying pans and kettles and big glass storage jars full of pasta.

"He won't want any of those," and Peter gave a little sigh.

Then, suddenly, behind the egg whisks and the soup ladles, Peter caught sight of something his brother would really like. So he took out his money and bought the present.

Next morning Peter's brother was delighted when he unwrapped his gift.

"These are just perfect for me!" he said with a grin.

You see, Peter's brother was a circus clown, and he had broken all his breakfast pots practising his tricks.

"My old cups and saucers were very plain and boring," laughed Peter's brother. "These are just what I need and I promise not to break them!"

"Come on," said Peter. "Let's have some breakfast!"

The Wasp That Flew Round The World

Wilf the wasp went on a journey. It wasn't a very long journey, although he flew round the world.

The other insects were really impressed.

"Our very own Wilf the Wasp has flown right round the world all by himself!" they buzzed. "How did you do it in such a short time?"

"Follow me!" cried Wilf. "And I'll show you!"

First Wilf flew over the lawn, twice round the rose bushes, in through the open window of Honeysuckle Cottage... ROUND THE WORLD...and out through the window!

"You tricked us!" mumbled the bumble-bee.

"So I did," hummed Wilf. "And now I'm going round the world again - but this time I shall land on Japan or Australia, or possibly Spain!" And off he went!

Monty The Mountie

One day Monty the Mountie got a very important phone call.

"As you are such a marvellous Mountie," said the Chief of all the Mounties, on the other end of the line, "I am sending you to the Great Whispering Pine Forest to keep a sharp look-out for desperate criminals.

I know you are the right man for the job," the Chief of the Mounties went on, "so good luck marvellous Monty Mountie!" And he rang off.

So Monty the Mountie packed his spare uniform and a map, and set off to find the Great Whispering Pine Forest.

Monty drove all day, and just before the sun set behind the mountain, he came upon a log cabin - his new post. Outside was a tall flagpole with the Mountie's special flag flying from the top.

"Here at last!" said Monty the Mountie, as he saluted smartly. "I'd better get unpacked and settled in before nightfall!"

Now Monty's log cabin was rather small, but it was warm and comfortable and had everything a Mountie needed.

"Tomorrow," yawned Monty, who was feeling very tired, "I shall begin my search for desperate criminals. But tonight I shall cook myself some pancakes with maple syrup, then go straight to bed!" So Monty set the table, popped a pile of fresh pancakes onto the warm plate and was just about to pour on the maple syrup, when there came a knock at the door.

"Do I smell maple syrup on warm pancakes?" a small voice asked.

And when Monty the Mountie opened the cabin door, he found a tiny chipmunk standing there.

"It's getting rather dark and cold outside," said the little fellow. "Can I come inside and have some supper?"

"Certainly!" smiled Monty, who was feeling a bit lonely. "I've made enough pancakes to feed the whole of the Great Whispering Pine Forest!"

"In that case," giggled the little chipmunk, "can my friend the rabbit and his friends the raccoons come in too?"

"Plenty of room and plenty of pancakes!" laughed Monty, and he opened the cabin door wide.

"How about me?" shouted a big brown bear as he lumbered out of the trees.

"Leave room for us!" called a couple of squirrels, and they scampered across the clearing and hurried into the cabin.

244

When at last Monty closed the door, he gazed across his ,cabin in surprise.

It was packed full of animals from the forest. Some were eating pancakes, others were drinking mugs of hot coffee, and one or two of the smaller animals had fallen asleep in front of the fire.

"Are you all staying the night?" asked Monty as he looked round and saw several beavers he hadn't noticed before.

"Yes please!" everyone replied, and begun getting ready for bed at once.

All of a sudden Monty the Mountie felt somebody tugging at his sleeve.

"Nobody wants to sleep near me!" It was a small skunk who had brought his own sleeping bag.

"How did you get in here?" gasped Monty, who by now couldn't find a place to sleep at all.

The little skunk looked very glum.

"I'll tell you what!" said Monty.

"We'll both sleep outside tonight. I'll light a camp-fire and we'll both be warm and cosy."

And so he did!

"Well, I'm certainly not going to be lonely in my new home," Monty sighed as he looked up at the night sky. "Although my new friends are not going to fit into my log cabin for long. Tomorrow I shall have to find them somewhere else to live!"

But that's another story ...

Pass The Parcel

The lifeboat crew had nothing to do one day. The weather was fine - no wind or rain, and the sea was calm and still.

"Everybody is being very sensible today," said one of the crew.

"No-one has dropped off to sleep on their air-bed and floated out to sea, and nobody has been cut off by the tide or been stranded on the rocks!"

Just then the postman arrived at the lifeboat station. "No letters today lads!" cried the postman cheerfully, and all the lifeboat men groaned.

"But there is a parcel, and it's addressed to all of you!" And the postman went on his way.

"I wonder what it is?" asked a lifeboat man. "Let's open it and see!"

"Wait a minute!" said the coxswain of the lifeboat. "As we have nothing else to do at the moment... Let's play Pass the Parcel."

All the lifeboat men cheered loudly.

"I haven't played Pass the Parcel since I was a little boy!" said one.

"Neither have I!" chuckled another. "But I can remember how to play - First everyone sits in a big circle, and when the music plays the parcel is passed round and whoever is holding the parcel when the music stops - starts to unwrap it."

"I'll be in charge of the music." said the

coxswain. "Come on lads, let's begin!"

Quickly the lifeboat men passed the parcel around, and one by one they tore off the wrapping paper.

"This parcel's getting smaller and smaller," said one of the crew.

"Soon there'll be nothing left!"

"I think this must be the last layer!" shouted one of the men as the parcel was tossed to him.

"Hurry up!" yelled the man next to him. "Pull the string and find out what's inside!"

... And find out what they did!

As the lifeboat man pulled hard on the string, there was a noise like air coming from a balloon ... and suddenly, in the middle of the circle, was a huge inflatable life-raft - growing bigger every second!

It gave the crew such a shock, that several of them fell over backwards.

"Come on, lads!" yelled the coxswain, switching off the music. "No time for games, let's go down to the shore and launch our new life-raft!"

Madeleine Brings The House Down

When Pierre played his accordion and whistled a tune, people loved to dance to the music.

Sometimes Pierre's wife Madeleine would sing along - now that was a different story!

Madeleine's voice was so high and shrill, that when she hit a top note, the noise would shatter glass!

She had broken all the windows in her house and cracked her best mirror too!

"I think your singing is simply beautiful," sighed Pierre as he played Madeleine's favourite tune on his accordion.

The more Madeleine sang, the more damage she caused. Houses began to shake, and chimney pots fell off buildings. Even the church spire began to look crooked when Madeleine sang nearby.

One day a gentleman asked Pierre if he would come and play his accordion in the street near his house.

Pierre agreed, and Madeleine came along to sing a song or two.

Halfway through the second verse of Madeleine's favourite french folk song, the gentleman began to beam with pleasure.

"It must be your beautiful voice," Pierre smiled at Madeleine. "Sing louder, dear!"

All of a sudden there was an almighty crash and the gentleman's house fell down!

"Thank you so much, Madeleine!" cried the gentleman as he kissed her hand. "My old house needed pulling down so I can build a new one - and you have demolished it for me with your incredible singing!"

Rosalind Learns To Read

The whole family was very proud when Rosalind learned to read. Grandma and Granddad ordered her a whole set of encyclopedias with lots of reading and hardly any pictures.

Mum and Dad went to the bookshop and bought Rosalind a whole pile of books about ponies and princesses and adventures on magic islands.

Rosalind read them all!

One afternoon when everybody was sitting together, Rosalind took out one of her books and opened it at the first page.

"Shall I read you all the story of the Princess and the Pea? the little girl asked, and everyone agreed that they would love to listen.

"Once upon a time... " Rosalind began - and she carried on until she had read the whole story.

"Would you like to hear another one?" asked Rosalind. So she picked up another storybook and began again.

Rosalind read another story, then another and another... and every one listened spellbound... or so Rosalind thought!

Dickie's Dragon

"There's a dragon in the garden?" said Dickie to his mother one day.

"How very nice, dear," murmured his mother, who was making a sponge cake at the time. "What does he look like?"

"He's scaly and green with a forked tail. His nostrils are enormous and he can breathe fire... but most of the time he just puffs out smoke!" replied Dickie, who always described things perfectly.

"How very nice, dear," said his mother as she watched her sponge cake slowly sink in the middle.

So Dickie went out to tell his dad.

"There's a dragon in the garden!" said Dickie.

"Has he got big feet?" asked his dad.

"Gigantic!" Dickie replied. "They're flat with three giant toes and long hooked toe-nails!"

"Then tell him to keep off my seeds!" said dad, without even noticing he was raking over the ground where the dragon had left his footprints.

"What did you say was in the garden!" asked dad.

"A dragon!" Dickie replied.

"Show me!" said Dad.

"He's gone now," said Dickie, "but you can see where he's been!"

Little Silver Stream's Secret

Little Silver Stream had a secret.
He had been busy for a whole week.

Early in the morning, he would creep
quietly past the Wigwams where
everybody was still fast asleep inside.
Then he would run swiftly until he came
to a bend in the river, where the mud
was soft and sticky -just perfect for
making pots.

Now Little Silver Stream had broken most of his mother's best pots - quite by accident, of course! So for a whole week he had been making new pots for her and drying them in the hot sun.

At last they were ready, and Little Silver Stream carried them carefully back to his village.

Now everybody wanted to know what Little Silver Stream had been up to, so they gathered round to take a look.

Sad to say, as soon as Little Silver Stream placed his pots on the table - they fell over, ...and you can see why!

Little Silver Stream had forgotten to make the bottoms of his pots flat!

The whole village laughed at Little Silver Stream, and the little boy hung his head in shame.

"What good is a pot that doesn't hold water!" someone shouted. "We should name you Little Silly Stream instead!"

Now Little Silver Stream's mother was very wise. Straightaway she went to the river and made several rings of clay. She left them to bake in the hot sun and went back for them the next day.

When she came home she placed each pot on top of a clay ring. They fitted perfectly and the pots didn't fall over.

Little Silver Stream and his mother filled their new pots right up to the brim with water.

"I love my new pots," laughed Little Silver Stream's mother, "because you made them especially for me!"

251

The Playboat

Fisherman Bill was fishing in the sea one day when his boat sprang a leak.

"Goodness me!" cried Fisherman Bill when he saw the size of the hole at the bottom of his boat.

"If I don't get a move on, I shall sink!" So Fisherman Bill rowed like mad, and reached the shore just in time.

"You're getting far too old to go out to sea fishing," said Fisherman Bill's wife as she helped him pull the leaking boat up onto the beach.

"You're quite right, my dear," Fisherman Bill agreed. "From now on I shall fish with my rod and line from the pier."

As Fisherman Bill's wife gazed at the old boat, she had an idea.

"I shall fill your old boat with pretty plants and flowers," she said with a smile. "It will look lovely in front of our cottage."

Fisherman Bill began to look rather worried because he knew he would have to water those plants at least twice a day - and he hated gardening!

"I have a much better idea," he said crossing his fingers, "I'll fill my old boat with sand, then all the children can bring their toys and play inside it!"

What a good idea!

Iggy Babysits

Iggy promised that he would look after all the baby frogs while the older ones went to a party.

"It won't be easy!" said Silver Minnow when he saw all the baby frogs jumping around.

"Nothing to it!" smiled Iggy. "I shall put them all in this old tin bath while I sunbathe. They'll come to no harm!"

So off went Iggy to sunbathe while all the little frogs simply leapt and jumped and bounced about all over the place.

I think Iggy may need a little help to collect all those bouncing babies, before their mums and dads return!

255

Don't Say A Word

Lyn and Lucas sat back to back in the garden, not saying a word.

Earlier that day they had been arguing and fighting. Now they refused to speak to one another.

Mother decided not to interfere, and went inside to put her feet up.

So Lyn and Lucas sat looking straight ahead, each one determined not to be the first to speak.

As Lyn gazed up into the sky, a small silver spaceship with a little green man on board circled overhead.

At the same time, Lucas happened to notice a gigantic blue genie appear from the spout of his dad's watering can.

But Lyn and Lucas sat back to back not saying a word.

Then along came a bright red dragon. It walked right past Lyn, followed by a knight in shining armour.

Was that the Queen in her cloak and crown, strolling on the lawn just in front of Lucas?

But Lyn and Lucas still sat back to back, not saying a word!

Suddenly, out of the long grass, crept a big hairy long legged spider. It ran across Lyn's bare toes and up Lucas's leg.

"Help!" screamed Lyn, jumping in the air.

"Get it off me!" yelled Lucas at the top of his voice.

"Oh good!" said Mother from inside the house. "Lyn and Lucas are speaking to each other at last!"

257

The Brown Teddy's Wish

"I think it's a shame," sighed the Brown Teddy Bear, "that we can't play with all of the toys when the children have gone to bed."

"But we can!" said Susie the doll. "We play with the bricks and the train, and we do a different jigsaw puzzle every night!"

"She's right!" added the Blue Monkey. "We play in the doll's house and use the tea-set. If you like we can all play 'Snakes and Ladders' tonight!"

"No thanks," sighed the Brown Teddy Bear, and went to sit in a corner by himself.

"I wish we could play in the pedal cars, just like the children!" said Brown Teddy

Bear. "Have you seen the way they race around, then crash into each other, with a BANG!"

"We can't do that!" the Blue Monkey replied. "It makes so much noise, it would wake the family.

"I know!" sighed the Brown Teddy Bear, and he went back to sit in the corner again.

However hard they tried, the rest of the toys could not persuade the Brown Teddy Bear to play with them. So night after night he sat alone in the corner.

Then, one day, something happened that changed things. The children who lived in the house came in from the swimming

pool and left their blow-up swim rings on the playroom floor.

"What are they for?" asked Susie the doll, are they a new kind of cushion?"

"Not exactly!" smiled the Blue Monkey. "They are full of air, which helps keep you afloat when you're learning to swim."

"They're not a lot of good to us then," remarked Susie the doll, and she ambled off to play dominoes with the finger puppets.

"Now you're quite wrong," said Blue Monkey thinking hard.

"Teddy," he shouted. "Come over here, I want to show you something!" He slipped the swim rings over the pedal cars.

The Brown Teddy Bear's eyes lit up at once. "Now we can race and crash into each other without a BANG!"

"No one will hear us," laughed Susie the doll. "Move over, Teddy, let me have a go!"

Underwater Fright

Iggy Frog and his best friend Silver Minnow were swimming along in the pond one day, when a long black shadow slowly passed overhead.

"Perhaps it's a duck or a moorhen," said Iggy as he looked round about him.

"Can't be' " called Silver ' Minnow as he darted left and right.

"We would have seen their webbed feet!"

All of a sudden Iggy Frog and Silver Minnow looked down, and there was the long black shape swimming beneath them.

"It's a PIKE!" gasped Silver Minnow, and both of them dived behind a rock for safety.

"Pike eat little fish like me!" whispered Silver Minnow.

"And frogs too!" croaked Iggy, quaking with fear.

As soon as the pike disappeared, the two friends swam as fast as they could to the safety of shallow water - for they knew the big pike couldn't follow them there.

"Did you see his sharp teeth?" cried Iggy.

"He's got rows and rows of them," sobbed Silver Minnow. "We'll never be safe in our pond again!"

"Why don't you give that pike the fright of his life?" asked an old water-vole who lived in a hole in the bank.

"How?" cried Iggy and Silver Minnow together.

"Easy!" replied the water-vole. "Paint the underneath of Iggy's yacht to look like a shark. That'll scare him away forever!"

So Iggy fetched his yacht, which was tied up in the reeds, and the two set to work.

As soon as the paint was dry, Iggy, Silver Minnow and the old water vole launched the boat into the pond and climbed aboard.

"Keep very quiet!" whispered the water-vole as he leaned over the side.

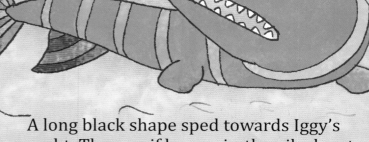

A long black shape sped towards Iggy's yacht. Then, as if by magic, the pike leapt out of the water and across the pond into a nearby stream.

Iggy and Silver Minnow watched him jumping in and out of the water until he was out of sight.

"He's gone for good!" laughed the old water-vole. "We certainly gave him a fright!"

Iggy and the Silver Minnow had to agree!

Paco Goes Shopping

Every Thursday morning, Emilio and his mother and baby sister Maria went shopping.

"My list is very, very long today!" said Emilio's mother with a sigh.

"Perhaps we could carry the shopping home on Paco's back," Emilio suggested.

That morning at the market, Emilio's mother bought lots and lots of shopping.

"Poor Paco will never be able to carry all those bags on his back," said Emilio. "He's far too small."

"Never mind," said his mother. "Paco can carry Baby Maria home, and I'll push the shopping!"

A Weekend Away

The toys had been invited to go to stay in a hotel for the weekend.

"Isn't it exciting!" squealed the dolls, and off they ran to sort out their best clothes.

"How will we get there?" asked the toy dog. "I don't think that any of the other toys have passed their driving test."

"I happen to be a very good driver," said Teddy, who was beginning to feel quite important.

"You'll all arrive safe and sound with me behind the wheel!"

The toys were busy all day long washing and ironing their best clothes, and filling their toilet-bags with toothpaste and clean flannels. A couple of the dolls decided to take their tennis rackets, and the pink rabbit thought it would be a good idea to pack his golf clubs.

"Are we going swimming?" asked the kangaroo.

Teddy thought they probably would go swimming, so all the toys packed their costumes and towels.

First thing next morning, they all gathered on the pavement outside with piles and piles of luggage.

"Oh, my goodness!" gasped Teddy. "There won't be enough room for all of you and your luggage too!"

One or two of the smaller dolls began to cry. "Don't leave us behind Teddy!" they pleaded.

"Now don't be silly," said Teddy kindly. "All of you have brought far too much luggage for just a weekend!"

So Teddy chose the biggest case of all and suggested that the toys just used that.

"This case will fit perfectly on top of the mini-bus, which leaves more room for you all inside."

At first the toys argued about who would take what, but at long last the big case was filled to bursting. The elephant sat on one side and a crowd of toys sat on the other, because that was the only way they could shut the case!

While all this had been going on quite a crowd had gathered. Other toys from down the street had come to see what was going on.

"It's a jumble sale!" one of them shouted to the others.

"No it is NOT!" yelled the rag doll, as she snatched her favourite dress from a big china doll who lived at the bottom of the street.

"Stop arguing and let's get a move on!" shouted Teddy as he walked towards the mini-bus.

"Wait for us!" cried the toys who were busy trying to rescue their belongings.

So the elephant, helped by the pink rabbit, gathered up all the extra clothes and carried them inside the house.

"We'll sort everything out after the weekend," said Teddy as he started up the mini-bus. He looked over his shoulder to check that all the toys had their seat-belts on, and off he went.

The rest of the toys from down the street were left looking rather puzzled as the mini-bus drove away.

Especially when the rag doll stuck out her tongue, and made a rude face at the big china doll who had tried to snatch her favourite dress.

261

The Robots Picnic

Ivor had a robot with a very strange name.

"My name is Ivor's Robot!" said the metal man, and that is what he became.

Now Ivor's Robot built himself a puppy. "His name is Spare Part, because that is what he is made of!"

One summer day, Ivor thought it would be a great idea to have a picnic outside under the trees.

"I shall bring the food and set the table," said Ivor's Robot. So off he marched towards the garage where all the tools were kept.

"Have you ever been on a picnic before?" Ivor asked his robot when he looked down at the food on the table.

"No never," said Ivor's Robot, and he shook his head. "I just brought the things I like to eat best and put them on the picnic table!"

So Ivor went inside to the kitchen, and brought out all the food he liked best too, and everyone tucked in and enjoyed the picnic!

Monty's New Village

Monty the Mountie woke up very early in the morning. The night before, lots of animals from the forest had come to stay in his log cabin.

There were so many in fact, that Monty and his new friend the skunk, had to sleep outside.

"I must find the animals somewhere to live," said Monty to himself. "And I must do it before the Chief Mountie pays me a visit. I'm supposed to be keeping a sharp look-out for desperate criminals, not looking after bears and squirrels and beavers... did I say beavers?" All of a sudden Monty had a brilliant idea.

Very gently he woke up a little beaver who had been sleeping in his log cabin.

"Do you have any brothers and sisters?" he asked the little fellow.

"No!" yawned the beaver, still very sleepy. "But I do have lots of aunts and uncles and I don't know how many cousins!"

"Excellent!" grinned Monty.

"Let's go and ask them to come over for breakfast."

So before the rest of the animals in the cabin were awake, Monty the Mountie and his little friend set off to find all the other beavers in the forest.

When Monty's jeep pulled up in the clearing by the river where the beavers lived, they had been up for hours. All of them were hard at work felling trees and building a dam.

"You look busy!" said Monty as he wandered over to the Head Beaver.

"Not a bit of it!" the Head Beaver replied. "We've nothing to do when we've finished this dam."

Now when the Head Beaver heard about Monty the Mountie's plan, he was very pleased.

All the beavers were eager to return with Monty and start work straightaway.

"There's nothing a beaver likes better than gnawing through logs all day.

He'll cut down your trees with the greatest of ease.

Give him some wood, and he'll stay!"

The beavers sang a song at the tops of their voices as they went back to Monty's cabin.

Now on the way they passed a lumberjacks' camp.

"I'll ask the Chief Lumberjack if I can borrow a bulldozer, and a couple of chainsaws," suggested the Head Beaver. "He's a good friend of mine and we often help each other out."

When at last Monty and the beavers arrived at the log cabin, all the animals were up and dressed and about to have breakfast.

As he tucked into scrambled eggs and toast, Monty the Mountie told them about his plan.

"All of you together, with the beavers' help, are going to build yourselves new homes. First of all we must make a little clearing in the forest, then you can put up your own small village right next to my cabin."

"When do we start?" cried the animals all at once.

"When I've finished my toast!" laughed Monty the Mountie.

The animals began to build their very own village straightaway.

They all worked really hard, and in a while everyone had a home of their own.

No-one was lonely any more, especially Monty the Mountie, who now had lots of new neighbours!